GHOST SNIPER

DAVID HEALEY

Intracoastal Media digital edition revised April 2021. Print edition first published 2014.

Cover art by Streetlight Graphics

BISAC Subject Headings:

FIC014000 FICTION/Historical

FIC032000 FICTION/War & Military

ISBN:0615945902

ISBN:978-0615945903

"Your task will not be an easy one. Your enemy is well trained, well equipped and battle hardened. He will fight savagely."

—General Dwight D. Eisenhower
    D-Day Message to the Allied Expeditionary Force

CHAPTER ONE

Omaha Beach • D-Day June 6, 1944

PING. The sound of the first bullet ricocheting off the armor plating made the men in the belly of the landing craft racing toward Omaha Beach realize that they were just minutes from going ashore. A few double-checked their gear. Some thought of home. Others began to pray.

The big guns of the battleships anchored just off shore had been softening up the German positions since before dawn, but the pounding of the artillery had looked and felt distant, like a summer storm on the horizon. The bullet was like the first rain drop. The storm was about to break.

Micajah Cole tightened his grip on the rifle he carried. He just hoped he got a chance to use it. He was a tall, lean man with oddly colorless eyes that could have been cut from quartz. You saw eyes like that in old Civil War photographs of Southern Confederates, and Cole's helmet did indeed have a Rebel flag the size of a poker card painted on it.

"We're sure as hell in for it," said Jackson, a big man at the front of the landing craft. He leaned over and tried to spit, but nothing came out.

Other men were seasick, from fear or the *thud, thud, thud* motion of the shoebox-shaped LCVP as it crashed into the oncoming waves, drenching them all with spray. Cole could taste the salt in his mouth. *Ping. Ping.* More bullets struck the armored front. The landing craft was awkward in the water, more cinder block than boat, but at least its armor plating shielded them from the German rifle and machine gun fire.

Then a shell from a German 88 mm gun screamed in and exploded no more than twenty feet away, nearly swamping the LCVP, but the sturdy craft bulled toward the beach. All around them, in the morning light, were hundreds of other boats like their own, running toward shore. The air smelled of seaweed and cordite.

"I'm glad I done wrote my parents last night," said a quiet, scared voice next to Cole. The voice belonged to Jimmy Turner. He was no more than nineteen, though with his baby face he looked younger, just a scrawny boy made scrawnier by the fact that he was loaded down with so much gear that he could barely stand: boots, jacket, rucksack with C-rations, wool blanket and shovel, steel helmet, a plastic-wrapped M1 Garand with 100 rounds of ammunition. He gripped the side of the LCVP to keep his balance.

"Christ almighty, Jimmy," said Jackson, glaring at him. "Are you telling us your mama can read? I thought all you people from the hills was just barefoot ignoramuses."

Jackson might have said more, but he noticed Cole looking at him, and he shut up, then directed his attention elsewhere.

"Why does he always got to be like that, Caje?" Jimmy wondered. Gentle as a mountain deer, Jimmy was always expecting people to be decent, even an asshole like Jackson. Jimmy was what the mountain people back home called *simple*, a bit too childlike and slow-witted for his own good, and so Cole had been looking out for him since boot camp. It was Jimmy who had painted the Confederate flag on Cole's helmet.

"Never mind him. We're going to have a whole lot more to worry about than Jackson in about five minutes. Listen up, now. Stay by me and keep your head down," Cole said quietly to Jimmy. "When the ramp comes down, get off as quick as you can, like a rabbit out of a hole. The water is going to be deep, so keep your feet under you and your head up. Then get on the beach. Look for something to get behind that will stop a bullet. You get there and wait for me, you hear?"

The kid nodded, and that was the last thing anybody had to say because the bullets were coming thicker now, beating against the landing craft like deadly hail and whining overhead. The engine kicked down a notch, and then another. The boxy craft stopped its forward motion, then bobbed up and down wildly in the surf.

Men stumbled and fell into one another, even though they were packed together. The sound of machine gun fire was very close now. Bullets and tracer rounds hissed and popped into the water all around them.

Someone yelled, "Go! Go!" and then the ramp splashed down.

A handful of men never even made it off the LCVP alive. A burst of machine gun fire hit the front ranks of men, several rounds killing Jackson instantly and knocking him back into Cole. He crouched low and grabbed hold of Jackson's pack, propelling his body forward. Bullets thudded into Jackson's body. At the edge of the ramp Cole shoved the body away and leaped to one side to avoid the tangle of men in front of him.

Cole landed feet-first, with Jimmy right behind him. The cold sea was a shock—and it was deep.

Nearly over his head. A wave swept over them and for a moment Cole couldn't hear or see a thing but the gurgle of the surf and the green sea all around him, punctuated by the white trails of bullets arcing down from the surface.

By some miracle he stayed on his feet, which is what saved him, because if he had tried to swim, the weight of his gear would have dragged him down and drowned him. His head came up in the trough between two waves and he gulped down some air before going under again.

He managed to get his legs moving forward. Jimmy was struggling beside him, too short to have gotten any air, drowning, and Cole grabbed hold of Jimmy's pack with one hand. The boy was too heavy. Cole dropped his rifle and grabbed Jimmy with both hands, hauling him up, up, so that the boy got a lungful of air before they both went under again.

Cole fought down panic as his nostrils and mouth filled with salty water. He was from the mountains and everything about the sea scared him. Even after all their training for the landing, jumping in and out of boats and wading across beaches, it seemed to him that the ocean had just one purpose, and that was to drown him. He had almost drowned once in a wintry mountain stream, and the memory of it made his heart pound to the point of panic.

But as with most bad situations, he knew that if

you kept your head, you at least had a chance. Cole held his breath and kept working them forward, struggling to keep his feet under him in the surf and current. Then the waves subsided and there was sky above him. He took another lungful of air.

Step by step, they moved out of the deeper water. Cole tried hard to ignore the bullets slashing the water around them. Some of the LCVPs had come in closer and were spilling their cargo of men closer to the beach. More men joined them, slogging through the breaking surf until it was only waist high, and then around their knees, and finally they were on the beach itself.

Where all hell had broken loose.

Between the water's edge and the German positions lay 400 yards of open sand, punctuated by anti-tank obstacles that resembled oversized jacks from a child's game, tangles of barbed wire, and bodies. He noticed that some of the bodies were alive, squirming across the sand as best they could, keeping their heads down. Others resembled ground meat, staining the sand around them red.

"All right, let's go!" An officer started waving everyone forward. "On your feet! Get—" A shell cut him in half, leaving his legs moving in place for a moment like a giant crab, until they toppled over.

Cole, Jimmy, and another soldier ran toward one of the anti-tank obstacles. There was a body slumped next to it. The dead soldier had an entrenching tool in his hands, and Cole grabbed it and dug up a little more sand. It wasn't much shelter, but on that open stretch of beach, it felt like the Alamo. Just a few feet away was another mound of sand, behind which sheltered a lieutenant and two more soldiers.

Keeping low, Cole chanced a look toward the German lines. He had never been in combat, but it wasn't the first time someone with a rifle had been trying to kill him. You didn't grow up in the mountains without carrying on a feud or two, not if you were a Cole.

But this battlefield was a world away from dodging some mean bootlegger with a deer rifle. He could just see the German position. Directly across from them was a German pillbox with a machine gun, pouring fire down the beach. He could more or less see the tops of three German helmets—the squad operating the machine gun.

He itched to have a rifle in his hands. If there was one thing Cole could do, it was shoot. He was the best marksman in his company—maybe in the entire 29th Division—but the United States Army did not have a separate sniper unit. So his talents hadn't been put to much use.

Unfortunately, Cole's M1 was now somewhere at the bottom of the English Channel. Not that a rifle with open sights would have done him much good at that range.

"What do you see?" asked the soldier who had taken cover with them. Curious, the soldier raised his head to get a look and a lucky round from the Germans took off the top of his skull.

Some of the blood splattered on Jimmy's face. The kid wasn't looking good. He was extremely pale, with a hint of green under the skin. "We ought to shoot back," he managed to stammer.

"I reckon it's too far to hit anything," Cole said.

"I'm goin' to try," the kid said. "Back home, if they was to ask me what I done after comin' all this way, I ain't goin' to say I kept my head in the sand, hidin' from them Germans."

Before Cole could stop him, Jimmy peeked around the base of the anti-tank post and squeezed off a couple of rounds. Machine gun fire kicked up the sand all around them and Cole dragged the boy back behind the post.

"Let me know next time you plan on killing yourself."

"Too late."

Then Cole saw that one of the rounds had struck the boy square in the chest. He rolled Jimmy onto his back and jammed a hand over the hole. There wasn't a lot of blood, but the hole was leaking pink foam. More foam bubbled out of Jimmy's mouth. Cole had hunted enough animals to know that Jimmy was lung-shot.

"Medic!" Cole screamed. Nobody came, and for all he knew, all the medics were dead.

"I'm scared of dyin', Caje."

"Don't be scared. You're just goin' home is all."

"You tell my ma and pa I done good over here," the boy said. He was now wheezing like a forge billows that had a hole in it. "I'm sure goin' to miss home. You know how in the mornin' it gets light real slow, and the birds wake up, and then the sun finally comes over the mountains."

"I know." Cole pressed harder against the hole in the kid's chest, trying to keep Jimmy's air from leaking out, but the pink foam was pouring out now.

"I'm goin' there now," Jimmy said. "I ain't on this beach no more. I'm goin' home to the mountains."

Knowing it was no use, he stopped pressing on Jimmy's chest and held the boy's hand instead.

"You go on home, Jimmy. It's all right."

And then the mountain boy died there on the beach, his last breath audible even over the sounds of explosions and gunfire and shouts. His dead eyes stared and Cole closed them, getting sand all over the boy's face in the process. He brushed it away as best he could.

Then he slumped back against the post. Bullets *thunked* into it from time to time. Cole scarcely noticed. It had been a long time since Micajah Cole had cried about anything, but he sobbed now until the tears ran down his face. With the tears, too, all the terror of the last few minutes seemed to come gushing out of him.

Jimmy had been like a little brother to Cole. That kid hadn't belonged here any more than a rabbit belonged in a wolf pack.

Cole swiped at the tears on his face, getting sand in his eyes, and blinked until things came back into focus. More landing craft were arriving. Two Navy ships had moved impossibly close to the beach, anchoring sideways, and they were firing their broadside at the Germans. But still the bullets and shells kept coming at them. As Cole watched, one of the LCVPs was hit and exploded in a geyser of water, twisted metal and bodies.

Cole lay there, deciding what to do. Until he had heard the first bullet hit the landing craft that morning, the invasion hadn't seemed real. The Germans hadn't seemed real, either, considering that he had never even seen one. Now Jimmy was dead. Cole hadn't really hated the Germans. But he sure as hell wanted to kill a few of them for Jimmy. The wind dried the tears on his face, leaving salty trails.

He looked around. He didn't even have a weapon. Jimmy's rifle was now clogged with sand and was just as likely to blow up in his face as shoot.

All around him on the beach were other clumps of soldiers, pinned down in the same way. He noticed a lieutenant nearby, and saw that he was holding a rifle with a telescopic sight. That was unusual, but an officer did have some leeway in equipping himself. Some chose pearl-handled revolvers, which made about as much sense against German machine guns as a cavalry saber. A sniper rifle, on the other hand—

Cole took a deep breath. At that moment, he realized he was about to live another sixty years, or less than sixty seconds. He jumped up and ran toward the lieutenant, diving headfirst behind the little barrier they had thrown up just when a machine gun burst churned the sand. A bullet clipped his boot but missed his actual foot.

"What the hell are you doing, soldier!" the lieutenant screamed at him. "It's no safer here."

"I know that, sir." He nodded at the rifle. "It don't seem like you're using that. Can you shoot?"

"Of course I can shoot!"

"Good enough to hit them Nazis yonder?"

"Maybe not that good."

"I reckon I can."

The lieutenant handed him the rifle. "Then you go right ahead, Private."

Cole checked the muzzle, and the bolt action of the Springfield rifle. Both appeared free of sand and seawater, which was something of a minor miracle.

Unlike the M1 he had been issued, this rifle was not a semi-automatic. But in Cole's experience, it was only one shot that mattered. The one that hit the target.

He eased himself around the side of the sand barrier until he could see the machine gun nest through the telescopic sight. The optics were quite powerful. The scope was at least a four power, making the Germans appear four times closer. While he had dimly been able to make out the German gunners before, they now seemed to be a few feet away. He could even see their faces, just visible above the rim of the concrete pillbox. He put the crosshairs over the helmet of the man behind the machine gun and fired. Through the scope, he saw sand kick up a few feet in front of the pillbox. The machine gunner never noticed Cole because his attention was on shooting anything that moved on the beach.

The rifle was sighted in for a closer range. All right, then. He took aim again, this time floating the crosshairs just above the helmet, and then squeezed the trigger.

Cole never really saw the bullet hit home. One moment the German was there, and the next he was gone.

Abruptly, the machine gun stopped firing. Another man moved to take the dead gunner's place. Cole shot him as well. He worked the bolt action again, took aim, and shot the third man in the pillbox.

He started to hand the rifle back to the lieutenant, who shook his head. "You hang on to that, soldier. Where's your unit?"

"Don't know, sir. Mostly dead, I reckon."

"Better stay with me, then. We're going to put that rifle to use." The lieutenant shouted loud enough to be heard by the men taking cover nearby. "Listen up! We have to get the hell off this beach or we're all going to get killed. Now let's move out!"

The lieutenant jumped up and ran forward toward the next anti-tank barricade. Cole ran after him. Again, it wasn't much shelter, but it was better than nothing. Other men surged forward all around them, finding what shelter they could, or simply throwing themselves flat against the sand after running ahead a few feet.

Up and down Omaha Beach, shells still burst overhead and machine gun fire kept up its deadly chatter. The sands were now a blood-soaked killing field. Cole had silenced the pillbox directly in front of them, so the men moved forward again, not even waiting for the lieutenant's order. They ran farther and faster this time, even with their waterlogged boots and gear.

Cole expected every step to be his last. Crossing the open beach, he had never felt so naked and exposed. Though the machine gun was silent, they were starting to take rifle fire from the Germans in the sand dunes. Gratefully, he threw himself down on the sand beside the lieutenant.

Cole looked through the sight and saw that a German squad was moving back into the pillbox. If the machine gun was manned again, the American soldiers moving up the beach would be chewed to pieces.

He was breathing too hard to take good aim. He needed something to rest that rifle on. He looked ahead, but there was nothing between them and the bunkers but a final stretch of open sand and curls of barbed wire. Cole shifted around and put the rifle across the lieutenant's pack.

"Hey!" The lieutenant started to get up, but Cole pushed him back down.

"Better hold still, sir, or we're all going to wind up dead."

The Germans did get off a burst from the machine gun, but Cole shot them in quick succession. Then he was up and running toward the dunes. He got as far as the barbed wire before throwing himself flat. The lieutenant had wire cutters, and he snipped a path through the wire. More men were moving up and doing the same.

The big guns up in the dune bunkers could not angle down far enough to fire at the Americans who had made it this close to the German positions, but they were taking plenty of fire from the troops in the bunkers, who were targeting Americans with their Mauser rifles and even submachine guns. One by one, Cole picked them off. He bought the lieutenant and the other men enough time to move through the field of barbed wire.

Then the lieutenant threw a grenade through the slit of a concrete bunker. There was a flash and bang of high explosive, and then the enemy guns fell silent. The tide of battle had suddenly changed on Omaha Beach.

The lieutenant looked back and waved Cole forward.

"Stick with me and keep that rifle handy," he said.

CHAPTER TWO

Supreme Allied Commander General Dwight D. Eisenhower lit another cigarette, sucked the smoke deep into his lungs, and studied the wall-size map in the operations center for what seemed like the millionth time.

The map portrayed the English Channel and the French coast at Normandy, with units and ships, even airplanes, indicated by cut-out shapes that were periodically moved about the map by smartly uniformed WACS. It might all have been mistaken for a classroom exercise if the mood in the room had not been so tense and somber.

Although he was surrounded by staff, Ike felt very much alone. Since the moment that he had given the order to proceed with the invasion, it was as if he inhabited a glass cocoon. A heavy, invisible load seemed to stoop his shoulders as he hunched over his cigarette. Ike could literally feel the weight of responsibility—it was as tangible to him as one of the heavy packs that his soldiers were carrying ashore in France. He knew it was the weight of thousands of lives that hung in the balance that June dawn, and perhaps the outcome of the war itself.

What bothered Ike was that after months of planning, and the tremendous effort of thousands upon thousands of men from his own staff down to the field officers and the soldiers themselves, nobody knew that Operation Overlord would succeed.

It was all an incredible gamble, though it was also a calculated risk. Ike was fascinated by the Civil War and often recalled the words of Confederate General Robert E. Lee: "It is well that war is so terrible, or we should grow too fond of it."

Though he was a brilliant strategist, Lee had ordered the tragic Pickett's Charge at the Battle of Gettysburg. Ike couldn't help wondering if he was now commanding a similar disaster.

There were probabilities and predictions, of course, but they were not particularly reassuring. Some estimates put casualties on D-Day itself as high as seventy percent for the airborne forces, meaning seven out of every ten men he had seen off yesterday afternoon were potentially going to their deaths. He sucked on the cigarette again.

As many as 12,000 Allied troops could be killed and wounded before the day was out. That would mean thousands of families devastated by the decisions he had made. It was enough to keep a man up at night, which could explain why Ike hadn't slept much, and looked it.

Ike and most of his staff had been living on coffee, cigarettes, hot dogs and the occasional drink —though he never poured more than two fingers of scotch. His mouth tasted like an ashtray the morning after a party, but he barely gave a thought to himself, exhausted though he was. He knew that even now, men were fighting and dying on the beaches. He tried to harden his heart to that fact, but the thought still wrenched at him. At this very moment, more men were being ferried across the channel, probably seasick and cold.

"Any word yet?" he asked.

"Reports say there is little resistance at Utah Beach, sir. However, the German defenses were stronger than expected at Omaha. We're having a hell of a time there."

"Casualty reports?"

The aide just shook his head. "No solid numbers yet, sir, but the machine guns on the heights are really chewing our boys up."

"God help them."

Ike was fully aware that he and his staff had planned the largest military invasion of all time. Like most generals, he was a student of military history, and the closest example he had found of a similar attempt had come in 1588, when the Spanish Armada had sailed to sack England. Ike was not comforted by the fact that the invasion had been disastrous due to storms and a spirited English defense. The Spanish had lost most of their ships and thousands of troops had drowned upon being shipwrecked on the craggy Irish coast.

But Ike was not King Philip sailing blindly into stormy seas with little more than a blessing of the fleet and a trust in God's Will being done. Operation Overlord had been meticulously planned. That planning had also taken place during the last year in utmost secrecy, for the Reich had spies everywhere. Great care had been taken to plant the seeds of misinformation and deceit about when and where the invasion would take place.

The Germans knew, of course, that an invasion was likely, and any schoolboy with a map could see that it would take place somewhere along the French coast where it fronted the English Channel. Using fake guns and troop trains, artificial radio traffic, and a campaign of false information, the Allies had worked hard to deceive the Germans that the landing would come farther north, at Pas de Calais.

Had the Germans taken the bait? Depending upon the answer to that question, the war in Europe could be won or lost by lunchtime.

General Rommel had been summoned by Hitler to reinforce the so-called Atlantic Wall as a defense against the Allies. Defending miles of coastline with a military that was increasingly being spread too thin was no easy task, but Rommel was highly capable. Ike had groaned at the aerial surveillance photos showing yet more defenses being built. It seemed that every day that passed, the Germans were able to strengthen their positions. The Allies' best hope was to keep the Germans off balance. Would the Allied invasion come at Pas de Calais or Normandy?

All night, reports had been coming in, starting with the results of the aerial insertion behind German lines. Now, waves of men were storming the beaches themselves.

The weather had not been cooperative. A winter invasion was out of the question on the stormy English Channel. Late May or early June seemed to provide the best opportunity for a smooth crossing. But there had been cool, cloudy, rainy weather dogging them all through the English spring. It needed to be clear enough that airplanes could not only drop their men accurately in France, but also for the Army Air Corps to provide support. The cloud cover had still played havoc with the drop and some of the pilots had missed their targets, scattering the 101st and 82nd Airborne over more than twenty miles. Confused and fragmented, they were now trying to join up across the tangled hedgerow country that made up much of Normandy.

The invasion very nearly hadn't come off due to the uncooperative weather. The original date in May for the invasion had come and gone, a postponement prompted by the wet conditions. Another such delay had very nearly followed in June. When the forecasters had finally predicted a tiny window of opportunity for the following day, Ike had given the order to go ahead.

"OK, we'll go," were the simple words uttered by Ike that launched the Allied invasion of Europe early on the morning of June 6th.

All the men were in place, already loaded aboard cramped landing craft or prepared to board their planes for Normandy. To stand them down would have smacked of defeat and blunted the edge of their readiness. The ruse they had worked so hard at to convince the Germans that the landing would come elsewhere could fall apart at any time. In fact, the way Ike saw it, there was no more time nor any option but the present.

And so the order had been given. Now there was

nothing to do but wait ... and pray. Ike smoked, watching the changing locations of the figures on the map, and tried to imagine what it must be like to be on Omaha beach that morning. The soldier in him ached to be there; the husband and father in him nearly wept at the thought of the battle raging at that very moment.

CHAPTER THREE

KURT VON STENGER slept until just past midnight. He had gone to bed unusually early, thanks to half a bottle of burgundy and a delicious rabbit stew. But he always had been a light sleeper, a trait that had helped keep him alive through several years of war, and something woke him in the night.

He lay very still and simply listened. Airplanes. Many, many of them, droning high overhead. And yet he did not hear the sound of bombs, which was puzzling.

Unfortunately, he knew they would not be Luftwaffe planes. The Allies had more or less dominated the skies, though there were still a few Junkers and Messerschmitts to keep the Tommies and Americans on their toes. But that many planes could only mean one thing—the Allies were up to something big.

He eased out of bed—the rich, red wine had been a good sedative, though now he found that it had given him a mild headache—but did not turn on the light. No point in giving the Allies a target, not even so much as the pinprick of light his bedroom window would make. Let them grope their way over France in darkness.

Though the night was cool, Von Stenger did not bother to dress, but only tugged on a silk smoking jacket and slid his feet into slippers. His bedroom was on the second floor off an old Norman farmhouse. It had been home to generations of gentry, and had some fine touches, such as the balcony off the bedroom that was a pleasant place to take his morning coffee.

He went out and looked up at the sky. The breeze had a cold, damp edge and there was a great deal of cloud cover because few stars were visible, but there was just enough ambient light for him to see that the night sky was filled with parachutes, creating a Milky Way of silk. Dimly, he could see them floating down as plane after plane roared overheard, spilling its cargo.

Von Stenger was not particularly alarmed or surprised. There had been rumors for some time of an Allied invasion. It was really only a matter of where and when, because the Americans and English needed some toehold on the continent. Tonight, they had finally come to Normandy.

He lit a cigarette—no Allied pilot was going to notice the glow of a Sobranie from that high up—and watched the parachutes float down. There were far too many jumpers for this to be another one of the British SAS's nuisance raids. No, this must be the start of something big. Already, far, far in the distance, he began to hear submachine gun fire.

With the gold-tipped cigarette dangling from the corner of his mouth, Von Stenger padded back into his room and returned to the balcony with his Mosin-Nagant rifle. This was a Russian rifle that he had taken off a dead sniper in the frozen rubble of Stalingrad, where Von Stenger had earned the nickname *Das Gespenst*—The Ghost—for his ability to slip silently through the ruins of the city, putting bullets into enemy snipers.

It was a rather battered weapon, but it was as familiar to Von Stenger as his own reflection in the mirror. The rifle had served him well in Russia. He could tell a story about each of the nicks in the stock and scratches on the barrel, though none of them would have been particularly good bedtime stories. They were perhaps more suitable as nightmares or horror stories.

His service in Russia had won him the Knight's

Cross. While Von Stenger was not an ardent Nazi—
he had little use for politics—he was very proud of
the medal at his throat. His experience in Russia also
earned him a stint teaching at the Wehrmacht's
sniper school, and the rank of captain. It was somewhat unusual for a sniper to be an officer—for the
most part, snipers worked in teams or were expected
to operate as *jaeger*—the German military tradition of
lone hunters or scouts. A sniper had no need to order
anyone around, and he generally did his duty without
needing anyone to tell him how to go about it.

Von Stenger came from an old German family
with friends in the right places, and they had seen to
it that he now wore a Hauptmann's insignia.

As one of the top snipers in the Wehrmacht, Von
Stenger easily could have procured one of the newer,
semi-automatic sniper rifles like the Walther K43.
But this rifle had taken him far. It was now like part
of him. He would not have traded it any more than
he would have willingly parted with an arm or a leg.

There was an old chair on the balcony that Von
Stenger sometimes sat in while he smoked. He pulled
it closer, sat down, and rested the rifle on the railing.
The parachutes were quite far, and it wasn't easy
finding them with the telescope, which offered a very
limited field of view. So Von Stenger picked out a
parachute with his naked eyes, and then keeping his
gaze on it, brought the telescopic sight up to his eye.

The parachute was now visible in the telescopic sight.

He took aim at the figure dangling at the end of the parachute harness, moving the rifle down to keep pace with the parachute as it settled lower, and squeezed the trigger. The parachute was much too far away to determine if the bullet had hit home, but it had certainly come close enough to give the airborne soldier something to think about as the bullet zipped past.

He picked out another parachute, took aim, fired. The parachutes themselves were much easier targets, but where was the challenge in that? Besides, a bullet hole was not going to bring down a parachute. He noticed that they drifted to earth in about forty seconds, which was plenty of time to pick out a target—sometimes two or three—from the same plane.

In the distance, small arms fire increased in intensity. Von Stenger smiled. He was not the only one giving the parachutists a warm welcome to France.

In the house below him, he could hear movement as the gunshots near and far brought the farmhouse awake. There would be no more sleep for anyone in the house tonight. The old farmer who owned the place had long since been taken away by the SS on suspicion of helping the *maquis*—the French Resistance—but his wife and daughter still lived there.

They kept Von Stenger and the other German officers billeted there well fed in the futile hope that it
would help the farmer's case.

He called for coffee, lit another cigarette, then
picked out another parachute. There did seem to be
an endless supply. More planes moved overhead,
emptying their cargo, the parachutists spilling out
like down from a milkweed pod.

As one parachute after another bloomed in the
sky, Von Stenger targeted them out and fired. Dawn
was still some hours away, but it was shaping up to be
a pleasant morning.

* * *

CORPORAL JAMES NEVILLE took off his steel helmet,
placed it on the jump seat, and then sat back down.

"Neville, what the hell are you doing?" asked
Dooley, who occupied the seat beside him. He had to
shout the words to be heard over the roar of the twin
1,200 horsepower Pratt & Whitney engines powering
the Douglas C-147 Skytrain bearing them aloft.

"Insurance," Neville explained. "When the Jerries
start up with their flak guns, I don't want me arse
shot off."

Dooley snorted, and shook his head. You could
always count on Neville to do something, well,
unusual. He was a bit gung ho, even for a paratrooper.

"We're about to jump out of an aircraft at low altitude behind enemy lines—at night, mind you—and you're worried about a random piece of shrapnel biting you in the arse?"

"It's best to be prepared for all contingencies," Neville said. He patted his front pocket. "I've even got a couple of rubbers in case my chute comes down in a brothel."

"In your dreams, Neville."

"A man can hope, can't he?"

That was the last they spoke, because the light flashed giving them the two minute warning to the drop site. Neville's stomach did a little flip-flop in time to the blinking light. Some of the men had actually vomited with fear and anxiety. Neville didn't blame them. The way Dooley had described what they were about to do made it sound, well, like a suicide mission. But they had trained again and again for this night. In other words, they had done it all before.

Some men now bowed their heads in prayer, but he didn't go in for that sort of thing. To keep his mind occupied, Neville went over his mental checklist. He had his rifle and ammunition, the standard-issue knife to cut his chute away once they landed, and rations.

He had added extensively to the basic equipment they had been issued. He also had a short, very sharp knife tucked into the top of each boot, a length of garrote wire wrapped around his canteen, a wrist-watch with a dial that glowed in the dark, and an American .45 automatic because he loved the fact it had been nicknamed "the flying ashtray" due to its slow, fat bullets. You couldn't hit a thing much more than twenty feet away, but if you did hit something with a lead ashtray moving at just under the speed of sound, you tended to knock it down.

He also had the rubbers he'd mentioned to Dooley, just in case any French girls showed special gratitude at being liberated. All things considered, he was about as prepared as any man could be to jump out of an aircraft into hostile territory.

Now the jump light stopped blinking and glowed with its steady, red light. The door to the aircraft slid open. If anyone's thoughts had been wandering, the sudden rush of cold night air brought them into sharp focus.

The men stood and silently attached the static lines that would automatically open their parachutes as they hurtled from the aircraft. Dooley was in line in front of him. They had all been through this so many times that there was barely any need for orders other than the jump master shouting, "Go, go, go!"

Then it was Neville's turn, and he tumbled out into the darkness. He positioned himself as he had been trained to withstand the sharp snap of the parachute deploying—it was a little like going off a diving board into a pool of nothing. They were jumping one after the other and he saw Dooley's chute blossom into a sudden puff of silk in the darkness. Then his own 'chute opened behind him with a sound like *whuff* and he was drifting with all the rest of the boys, the ground coming up fast.

He strained to see the landing zone. The area had been mapped carefully. The intent was that they would land in open fields. But the fields were ringed with trees, so that landing required a bit of maneuvering. Neville saw branches reaching up at him and pulled the cords to spill some of the air from his parachute to bring him down even faster, before he could drift into the trees at the edge of the field.

Something zipped past his head and a distant part of his mind thought *bullet*, but he was too busy trying to miss the trees to dwell on the fact that he was being shot at. He hadn't seen a muzzle flash or heard the report of a rifle over the roar of wind in his ears, so the shooter must have been far away.

He missed the field. The trees clawed at him, attempting to snag him, and he swung his legs up like a child trying to go higher on a swing. A branch snatched at the seat of his pants, but he kept out of the worst of the branches. Then he was coming down again, dodging a hedge, and the ground came up so hard that it seemed to swat Neville out of the sky. He was spinning a bit and going sideways, so he was disoriented. He rolled and rolled just as he had been trained, breaking his fall as much as possible. He came to a stop and took stock.

All right then, Neville old chap, you seem to be in one piece. Rapidly, he began struggling out of his parachute harness. He stayed down on his knees to present a small target, just in case any Jerries were out and about with their Mauser rifles. But aside from that bullet while he had been in the air, he didn't hear a sound. So far, so good.

He gathered up his parachute and ran to the edge of the field, where he stuffed the tangle of silken fabric and ropes deep into the brush. In the starlight, he could see that he had come down in a small field that appeared to be ringed by high hedges. A crop of wheat was just barely ankle high this early in the growing season.

He appeared to be alone, which was a good sign in some ways—no German soldiers about—but neither were there any British troops visible. That was definitely not part of the plan. There were supposed to be at least some men nearby. These groups of men were to join up into squads, and then the squads would become platoons and regiments to become a genuine fighting force. Looking up, Neville could see more parachutes coming down, but much too far away from his own drop zone. He could hear a distant rifle, measured and deadly, firing at them. Probably the same Jerry who tried to do for me, he thought.

Scattered about the French countryside, it might take the British countless hours to find each other.

It's all a bloody cock up. In Neville's experience, almost every large military operation had that very outcome, which was why he had paid so much attention to his own training. The knives, garrote and the .45 were added insurance.

He started off through hedgerow country, hoping to find some of his own troops to join. But if he did not, Corporal Neville was fully prepared to be a one-man fighting force. He clicked off the safety on his rifle and started trudging toward the sounds of firing.

If it was a fight the Jerries wanted, it was a fight they were bloody well going to get.

CHAPTER FOUR

WHEN LIGHT BEGAN to fill the sky, Von Stenger finally got up from the chair on the balcony and stretched. The rain of parachutists had stopped some time ago. It was hard to say how many he had shot, but the stone floor of the balcony was littered with cigarette butts and brass casings.

On a small table nearby were the leavings of his breakfast—an empty coffee cup and crumbs from what had been a rather delicious omelet with fresh bread and butter. If this war had kept up the way it had been going, he would have gotten fat. So very different from Russia, where the men had resorted to boiling their leather belts into a kind of soup to keep from starving. Von Stenger had been one of the fortunate few to escape that hell on earth, mainly because he'd had the good luck to suffer a minor wound that got him sent home to recuperate.

He thought back to Russia. All that snow and cold. What a disaster that had been. He sighed. *Der Führer* had been convinced that the Russians could be beaten. They were nothing but peasants. Well, Hitler should have asked a few of his men in the field about that. The Russians were anything but beaten. They were indeed peasants, but they were wily. Soon enough, they would be advancing on Berlin. Von Stenger knew it with certainty the way he knew the tide would come in.

He gazed at his empty plate and sighed. He could have done with another slice of bread and butter.

As if reading his thoughts, Willi Gault came in with a pot of coffee—and a bottle of calvados, Normandy's famed apple brandy. Gault was assigned to the engineer corps and he did not look at all like a soldier. He wore round spectacles, was balding, and his rotund figure indicated that he had partaken well of the regional French food. Von Stenger liked him because he was a good and competent officer.

"I see you have been getting in some target practice," Willi said, kicking at the spent shell casings. "Were you able to stop the invasion?"

"I don't think so," Von Stenger said. "But it was entertaining. Like shooting geese."

"I always favor shooting at things that can't shoot

back," the engineer said with a chuckle. He poured them coffee and calvados. "So, this is it. The long-awaited attack on the Atlantic Wall."

"Will it hold?"

Hitler and the German High Command had long praised the so-called Atlantic Wall, the ring of coastal defenses protecting France. It had been part of Willi's task to improve and strengthen these defenses, but Von Stenger felt he could ask without insulting his fellow officer. Only recently, Field Marshall Irwin Rommel had been brought in to oversee the coastal defenses. While Rommel had made many practical improvements, there was a vast coastal area to defend and a dwindling number of troops to do so.

"We are told it will stop an invasion." Willi shrugged. "Who knows?"

They both knew propaganda did not stop bullets or enemy troops. Von Stenger had seen as much in Russia. Both men sipped their brandy and drank their coffee. Willi topped off his own glass of calvados, but Von Stenger shook his head. In the distance, the deep roar of naval guns had begun. The coast was only two miles distant as the crow flies and the pounding of the guns shook dust loose from the ancient walls of the farmhouse.

"Ah," said Willi. "The bombardment begins. Next they'll be sending in the landing craft. It is going to be an ugly day." He drained his glass and stood. "Well, I'm off to the beach."

Von Stenger raised an eyebrow. "What? You'll be driving right into the bombardment. I would not recommend it."

Willi shrugged. "They will expect me there. Anything less would be cowardice. Listen, Kurt, I have a driver, but I think I'm going to leave him behind this morning. It doesn't make sense for us both to ... go. He's just a boy, really. I wondered if you would take him on?"

The sniper was surprised. "What am I going to do with a driver? I don't have a car!"

"Surely you need someone to carry your gear."

"I don't think I'd be doing him any favors, Willi. I'll be going into the bocage to fight the Americans."

"They'll be putting him into the front lines, then, and somehow I think his chances will be better with you." Willi seemed to consider, sighed, then poured himself another calvados, filling the glass to the brim, and drank it down. He offered his hand, and the two men shook. "Good luck to you, Kurt. It has been good knowing you."

Then Willi left the room, a little unsteadily. He was not normally such a big drinker. A few minutes later a car started in the courtyard below, and drove off toward the sound of the bombardment.

Von Stenger listened to it go and thought, *Good luck, old friend.*

Von Stenger dressed in field gear and then packed quickly and efficiently, putting just a few essentials such as spare socks into a haversack. Normandy was not Russia—and thank God for that—but the nights would be cold and miserable with wet feet.

He packed a small book of Goethe's verse and, after a moment's hesitation, a bottle of particularly good French burgundy that he had been saving, perhaps to drink with Willi some night. There was no reason to save it anymore, and he'd be damned if he was going to leave it for some soldier from New Jersey to guzzle. As Goethe would say, "Enjoy when you can, and endure when you must." Von Stenger decided it would be far easier to endure some future cold, rainy night with a bottle of good red wine. He topped off the haversack with a thick wool blanket, tightly rolled.

He and Willi had not finished the calvados, so he went out and poured what was left off the balcony. No point in leaving it for the American marauders to polish off.

The house felt empty, because the other engineers billeted there were already at the beach, and the mother and daughter of the house had fled to the nearby village. He made his way down to the kitchen, whistling, and was surprised to find Willi's driver sitting at the table, wolfing down coffee, bread and butter. He was baby-faced and his uniform was a bit too big for him, so that he looked more like a schoolboy than a soldier. He understood why Willi had left him behind—he was just a boy, and the engineer had been driving toward certain death. On the other hand, Von Stenger was not sure the boy would fare much better in the days of fighting to come.

"You are coming with me," he told the young soldier, who jumped to his feet at Von Stenger's arrival. "Pack your haversack and meet me back here in five minutes."

Von Stenger was amused to see that the boy took the time to salute before racing off. Who said that replacement troops had no discipline?

The kitchen was well stocked and Von Stenger collected canned meat, some fresh bread and a jar of jam, even some chocolate. Then he divided the food items into two piles; one went into his haversack and when the boy returned he told him to pack the other half.

The sky was brighter now, and the sounds of fighting coming from the coast were constant. Explosions from the Allied bombardment flickered on the horizon like distant fireworks. The deep boom of the Navy guns rattled the windows. A fine dust filled the kitchen as the ancient walls vibrated.

He noticed that the boy was white faced. Well,

only a fool wouldn't be scared at the thought of thousands of Allied troops trying to come ashore just a short distance away. It would be nice to think that the defenses would hold, but Von Stenger was sure the Americans and British and Canadians would keep coming until they finally captured the beach. In any case, he was certain that the surf would run red before the day was through.

He started off through the fields, with the boy following him. Apart from the distant thump of artillery, they might have been heading into the woods for a camping trip. The boy marched along deferentially a few paces behind and to Von Stenger's right.

"Sir, are we joining up with another unit?"

"We are a unit. I am a sniper, and you are my scout. What is your name, anyhow?" he asked the soldier.

"Fritz, sir. Matthias Fritz."

"Well, Fritz, there are a few simple rules to follow if you wish to stay alive out here. The first is that you always do what I say without question, and do it immediately. The second rule is to keep your eyes open at all times. It seems quiet now, like we are just out for a stroll in the fields, but you saw those paratroopers coming down. There is a lot more out here now than rabbits and foxes. The third rule is not to walk so close to me because two men make a more inviting target than one." Von Stenger stopped walking and stared at the young soldier. "*Schütze* Fritz, where is your rifle?"

"I, uh, I do not have one, sir. I am a driver."

"Perhaps I should shoot you now and spare the Amis the trouble. Every soldier must have a weapon."

"Yes, *Herr Hauptmann*."

Von Stenger started off again. "Well, don't fret, soldier. A boy like you probably won't live until nightfall. So try to enjoy your last day alive."

CHAPTER FIVE

Von Stenger moved deeper into the hedgerow country surrounding the farm. Despite what he had said to Fritz, he was not particularly worried about running into enemy troops.

Judging by the way they had come down in such scattered fashion in the early morning darkness, they would be trying to join up and figure out what the hell they were doing. In other words, the Allied forces would be highly disorganized. But Von Stenger had been fighting since 1938, first in the Spanish Civil War, then in Poland and Russia. He did not take survival lightly or for granted.

He considered the purpose of the airborne troops. It was obvious that the invasion taking place at the beach was to bring ashore vast numbers of men, tanks, trucks, and other materiel. Why had a relatively small number of men been parachuted into Normandy itself? Even a few hundred enemy troops might be no more than a diversion intended to wreak havoc, but surely they must have certain key objectives in mind.

Towns, he thought. Bridges. Roads. Rail lines. Yes, the Allies would be seeking either to gain control of these keys to transportation, or to destroy them.

From their present position, the nearest key target would be the bridge at La Profonde. And so he led Fritz in that direction.

Within an hour they were in view of the bridge. Von Stenger told the boy to wait, shed his haversack, and crept through the underbrush on a bluff above the bridge. Sure enough, the bridge was swarming with enemy troops. He could see a few dead Germans down below, all laid out in a neat row. Well, that was something—the Russians wouldn't have bothered with that nicety. The dead troops must have been the detail assigned to protect the bridge, or possibly couriers who'd had the bad luck to run into the Americans. They would not have had a chance against so many.

"Fritz, leave your haversack and come here," Von Stenger said quietly. "Move slowly. So far you have been rather useless as a soldier, but you can do that much, I expect."

The boy did just that, advancing until he lay in

the underbrush alongside Von Stenger. Von Stenger had a pistol, which he drew and handed to the boy. Fritz hesitated before taking it. "Sir?"

"You are my scout, remember? It is best for a sniper to work as part of a two-man team," Von Stenger explained. "This is as good a position as any. We have effective cover, and occupy relatively high ground above the bridge, which gives us a vantage point."

"Won't they shoot back?"

"This is a war, boy. Of course they will shoot back. However, they appear to be armed with automatic weapons, which don't have much range. Also, it is unlikely that they can flank us or get behind us because we can see their movements. They hold the bridge, it is true, but now we make them pay a price for it."

"Do you want me to shoot at them with this?" The boy waggled the pistol.

"You truly are a *Dummkopf*. From this range, you might as well throw rocks at them as fire a pistol. No, as the scout your job is to guard our rear. My attention will be on the men at the bridge. There is no telling who might be behind us. Go back to where we left the packs. If someone does come up behind us, shoot him."

Fritz gulped. "Yes, *Herr Hauptmann*."

The boy moved off, and Von Stenger turned his

attention to the troops around the bridge. It was clear that they were planning to hold the bridge rather than destroy it because no charges had been placed that he could see. He counted at least fifty men spread out around the bridge. Some had out their entrenching tools and were digging defensive positions. Von Stenger was pleased to see that their focus was on the road leading to the bridge on both sides of the river. Clearly, if there was to be a counter-attack, the Americans expected it to be from the road.

Located here on the high ground above the river, Von Stenger felt that he was in a strong position. He had good cover in that he was shooting from behind the bushes on the ridge—it was very unlikely that the Americans would see him or his muzzle flash, particularly not in daylight. If someone did come up behind them, the boy would at least get off a warning shot or two.

The Americans were maybe 200 meters away, which was a relatively easy shot. He picked out the man who seemed to be giving orders, put his crosshairs on the officer's chest, and squeezed the trigger. The man crumpled.

As Von Stenger had expected, the Americans below scrambled like ants, running for cover. One or two fired wildly, but the shots came nowhere near Von Stenger's position. He picked out a man hunkered behind a heavy machine gun in a foxhole commanding the causeway and shot him. A sergeant was his next target. Von Stenger fired again and again.

The Americans had no idea where the firing was coming from. They were learning a lesson that Von Stenger already knew very well, which is that it is very difficult to pinpoint the location of a single rifleman firing isolated shots. The breeze carried the sound away, and the echo of the shots made them seem as if the bullets were coming from several directions. At one point, the Americans spread out as if they thought they were surrounded.

Von Stenger smiled. Like babes in the woods. It was clear that these men never had been under fire. The Russians wouldn't have been so confused. At the very least, they would have had the good sense to keep their heads down. A sniper wasn't much use if he had nothing to shoot at. The Americans, however, were slow to learn their lesson.

Next, Von Stenger picked out another officer who seemed to be trying to establish some order among the men. At 200 meters, the four power scope made his face spring clearly to Von Stenger's eye. He was a young man with strong cheekbones beneath the shadow of his helmet. He could have been German, if not for the olive drab uniform. The sniper shot him through the temple.

Though they were slow learners, after that, the

Americans finally kept their heads down. He stopped firing and waited them out.

After a few minutes of silence, he heard Fritz moving toward him. "What's going on?" the boy asked. He looked white as a sheet. "Are they all dead?"

"Fritz, if you leave your post again against orders, I will shoot you," Von Stenger said. "Now go back and guard the rear like I told you to do."

"Yes, sir."

Von Stenger sighed as Fritz moved off. At that moment, it became clear to him that Germany was going to lose the war. The boy was too young and improperly trained. He knew very well that the ranks of the troops defending the Atlantic Wall now under attack were much like the boy, or conscripts from Poland and Russia. In other words, they were not reliable German troops. Conscripts and boys could never be counted on to fight real battles. Until that morning, Von Stenger had still held out some hope of victory. The best Germany could hope for now was that Hitler might negotiate some settlement with the Allies.

He reflected that this was much like a game of chess in which one had made a fatal error, and yet it was too early to give up. One's opponent might still make some foolish mistake. Some brilliant move might still present itself and thus save the game.

Down below, near the bridge, some soldier's helmet edged above the rim of his foxhole. Von Stenger put a hole in it. An instant later, a bullet nicked through the bushes not far from his head.

He had fallen for the oldest trick in the book. Some soldier had lured him with an empty helmet so that he would fire and reveal his position.

He pressed his eye more tightly to the telescopic sight. *There*. He could see a soldier in another foxhole nearby scanning the bank where Von Stenger was hidden. Fortunately, the American did not have a telescope mounted on his rifle. These were airborne commandos equipped with light automatic weapons intended for close fighting. It was an odd sensation, being able to see the man clearly even as he tried to see *him*, but could not. Von Stenger took aim and shot him. One could not have the enemy thinking they were real snipers.

This time, a few more shots tore into the brush, but by then he had melted away. The first rule of being a sniper was to change one's position frequently, to maintain the element of surprise and uncertainty. Once the enemy knew where you were, you were as good as dead. It was only a matter of time before they picked you off.

At least a dozen American bodies lay sprawled on the ground beside the line of German dead.

Welcome to the war, Von Stenger thought.

CHAPTER SIX

Omaha Beach • D Plus 1

"HEY, WATCH IT, BUDDY!" Lieutenant Mulholland turned just in time to dodge a detail that was carrying a wounded man toward the makeshift hospital set up on the beach. The medic, who looked dog tired, noticed his rank and muttered, "Sorry, sir."

Mulholland trudged up the beach, the heavy, wet sand clinging to his boots with every step. Some of the sand was stained red in patches. He was so bone weary himself that he hadn't even noticed he was walking into the path of the medical team. The poor bastard in the stretcher was covered in several places with blood-soaked bandages. He'd be going onto a launch to be carried out to one of the hospital ships, and from there to England—if he made it.

Considering that the wounded soldier was still breathing, he was better off than the dead men who were literally being stacked in the backs of trucks for removal from the beach. They would be buried further inland in a makeshift cemetery.

Mulholland tried to estimate the number of dead, but quickly gave up. God knew how many there were. Hundreds. Maybe thousands. He looked away. Much of his own platoon was part of the butcher's bill for taking the beach. Most of them died in seconds as machine gun fire poured into their landing craft when it hit the beach. He saw their faces, imagined the last letters home they had written in the hours before the invasion. What an utter waste of life, thanks to Adolf Hitler.

Mulholland felt guilty about it, but he was glad to be alive. Of course, there was a great deal of fighting yet to come. Who knew if he would survive? He could hear the *whump* of heavy guns a couple of miles inland. The Germans had lost the beach, but rumor was that they were fighting for every inch of country-side. Normandy's endless fields ringed by tall hedgerows made for a completely different kind of fighting.

Everywhere he looked, men and materials were in motion, with more swarming ashore at every moment. Stacked boxes and crates awaited transit off the beach. Tanks and trucks bulled their way through the surf and up onto the sand. The beach head estab-lished here was now the gateway to Europe. Through this portal would begin the liberation of France and Europe, until the Allied troops were at Hitler's door step. The sight of all the gear and men coming ashore somehow reassured him that the men on his landing craft had not died in vain.

While gunfire could be heard not so far off, the army bureaucracy had already established itself on the beach. Under a rough canvas sheet that flapped in the wind, typewriters had been set up on crates, where clerks were busy typing dispatches and keeping records of the material coming ashore—and of the dead. Telephone lines snaked from the clerical area into the dunes and countryside beyond. As Mulholland watched, two engineers were busy unrolling another spool of telephone wire. The clack of typewriters, the sight of telephone wires—it all seemed shockingly pedestrian after the carnage and sheer terror on the beach yesterday.

The lieutenant had been summoned to brigade headquarters for the 116th Infantry. He knew that being called to headquarters was never a good sign. It usually meant that you had screwed up somehow—or worse yet, that you were being singled out for some kind of special duty. Although he wasn't looking forward to what awaited him, he marched resolutely toward HQ.

The beach remained a combat zone, and so HQ was nothing more than a canvas tarp that had been rigged to keep off the rain and wind. More of the now ubiquitous telephone lines ran toward it. Sandbags had been stacked around the tarp to create a barrier, behind which a machine gun was set up in case of counterattack, although the likelihood of the Jerries recapturing the beach faded by the hour. He soon found himself standing before a harassed-looking colonel.

"Lieutenant Mulholland reporting, sir." He brought himself to attention and saluted.

"At ease, Lieutenant," the colonel said, returning the salute. The colonel was trying without much success to light a cigarette in the breeze off the ocean, also hampered by the fact that his left arm was heavily bandaged. Mulholland hurried to hold the military-issue lighter for him. "Thank you, son. You know, I used to like the beach, but I don't believe I'd care to spend a day at the beach again. I've got sand in cracks I didn't know I had."

"I know what you mean, sir."

"Well, it's our beach now, which is goddamn something. We paid a heavy price for this real estate, Lieutenant. And the Jerries are making us fight for every foot inland. Let me be clear that they are not in retreat but are fighting a defensive battle. The interior is nothing but fields, hedgerows and trees, and it's crawling with Germans. They've got tanks, artillery, snipers, and they're highly organized. The bastards are stubborn."

"Yes, sir." Mulholland wondered why the colonel was telling him this, which seemed to be something that everyone already knew. The colonel seemed to be leading up to something, which the lieutenant suspected would involve him and the reason he had been summoned to HQ.

"Like I said, the whole goddamn Cotentin Peninsula is lousy with Germans. Our own armored units can handle the Panzers and all the rest. But I have to say that the snipers are tearing us up pretty bad. We hadn't really counted on that. They're sneaky, cowardly bastards, but we need to adopt some of the same tactics if we're going to fight back. And that's where you come in, Lieutenant."

"Sir?"

"I understand that you worked with a sniper in the fighting yesterday to eliminate German resistance."

"We were just kind of thrown together, sir."

"Be that as it may, son, you are now the 116th Infantry's resident expert on sniper warfare." The colonel clapped him on the shoulder, then winced. "Damn, this arm hurts. Got to get it tended to. Listen, you've heard of an ad hoc committee? You are now in charge of an ad hoc squad. Your assignment is to eliminate as many of the German snipers as possible. Counter sniper warfare."

"I understand, sir. But—"

"Is that fellow you teamed up with yesterday still alive?"

"I believe so, sir."

"Good. Round him up. He's now part of your squad. I understand he's quite a shot. That's just what we need."

"So it's just us two, sir?"

"Hell, no, son. I'm way ahead of you there. I talked to the company commanders and got their crack shots. Either that or they were lying to get rid of a pain in their ass. Well, they're yours now. I even got you a guide. She claims to be with the French Resistance, so I suppose you can trust her. She's also easy on the eyes, I have to say, so that's a bonus."

"Why do I need a guide?"

"Let me paint you a picture, Lieutenant. The country all back beyond here is nothing but fields." The colonel waved his good arm in the general direction of the countryside beyond the beach. "The French call it *le bocage*, which means hedgerow country. I'd call it a goddamn nightmare. The Germans have it mined, booby trapped, defended with machine gun nests and snipers. It's ideal defensive ground, and unfortunately we've got to fight our way through it. Your mission, Lieutenant, is to make my job easier by eliminating as many of these German snipers as possible."

"Yes, sir."

"You and your men will be equipped with the Springfield sniper rifle. It's got a scope on it but it's a bolt action rifle. It's not as good as what the Jerries have, from what I understand, but it will get the job done. For the most part, the Germans have a lot more firepower than we do. They are very well equipped."

Mulholland nodded. He'd given his own sniper rifle to Cole yesterday, and it was clear that the man knew how to use it. Mulholland had equipped himself with the rifle because no one else in his unit had been particularly proficient, and being a couple of rifles short, he'd rather have one of the men get the semi-automatic M1 Garand. In Cole's hands, the bolt-action rifle had proven more than effective.

"Once you step off the beach, you're on your own. Work your way through the bocage country and reconnect with the 116th at St. Lo. Any questions?"

Mulholland had several, but he knew better than to ask. In the Army, it paid to act as if everything made perfect sense. "No, sir."

"Good. Then let me introduce you to your guide." The colonel led him toward a group of civilians. One glance told him they were French—the first French people he'd seen so far. Most of the men seemed to be wearing suit coats and berets, and smoking ciga-rettes. All of them had weapons slung over their shoulders or within reach. Mostly, they were equipped with hunting rifles, but there were a few deadly looking Sten guns among them. They were a hard-looking bunch and they studied Mulholland with flat grey eyes.

"I'm glad they're on our side, sir."

"Resistance fighters," the colonel muttered to Mulholland. "*Maquis*. They've been fighting the Germans since 1941—wrecking trains, spying on troop movements, cutting throats."

One of the Resistance fighters stepped forward. Though wearing trousers and a beret like the men, this one was most definitely a woman. She had high cheekbones, dark hair, and soft brown eyes. The colonel had been right about her being a looker.

She stood for a moment, checking him out, smoking a cigarette with one hand while the other hand cupped her elbow, forearm across her belly. "Jolie Molyneux," she finally said, exhaling smoke. *"Je suis heureuse d'être votre guide. En d'autres termes, je vais essayer de ne pas vous faire tuer, même pensé que putain douteuse."*

Mulholland attempted a smile. He looked to the colonel for help, but it was clear the man hadn't understood a word. His own high school French was so rusty it creaked, so all he could manage was,

"*Bonjour, Mademoiselle Molyneux.* I'm afraid I didn't understand what you said. Uh, *comment allez-vous?*"

His guide sucked deep on her American cigarette, exhaled. "Do not worry, Lieutenant, I speak English. What I said was, I will be your guide, but we are probably screwed."

Mulholland blinked. "Oh."

"There you go, son," the colonel said. He gave Mulholland a hearty clap on the shoulder. "Get your men together and move out as soon as possible."

"Yes, sir." He saluted.

The colonel moved off, leaving him with the Resistance fighters. Looking around at them, Mulholland couldn't help but wonder what the hell he and rest of the 29th Division were doing in France. It wasn't exactly a warm welcome.

"The first rule of sniper warfare is not to salute anyone," his new guide said in a matter of fact manner. "Not unless you want to get them shot. Snipers target the officers"

"I'll try to keep that in mind, *Mademoiselle* Molyneux. Now if you'll excuse me, I'm going to find my men."

CHAPTER SEVEN

MULHOLLAND FOUND the sniper right where he had left him not long after dawn. He was eating some kind of stew out of a tin cup, his rifle propped up nearby. There was something watchful about the sniper, as if he were sizing you up the way that a fox eyes a rabbit. He made Mulholland uneasy. He didn't bother to salute or stand—it was clear he didn't have much use for officers.

"That was some shooting you did yesterday," Mulholland said. "I never did catch your name, soldier."

"Cole."

"My name's Mulholland. Get your gear together and come with me," the lieutenant said.

Cole simply nodded, not bothering to *yes, sir* him.

He finished off the stew in two or three unhurried bites, wiped out the cup, and got to his feet. They'd been so busy yesterday killing Germans—and trying to stay alive while they were at it—that Mulholland hadn't really gotten a good look at Cole. He did so now. The sniper was not a particularly tall man, definitely shorter than Mulholland, but he was so lean and wiry that he gave the illusion of being taller. Though young, he looked tough and weather beaten, like a piece of oak root or a leather belt that had gotten wet and been left in the sun to dry. Nothing soft or citified about him. Up close, he looked mean and tough.

Yesterday, Mulholland had noticed that there was a country twang in the sniper's voice, some kind of hillbilly accent that came from someplace deep and old back in the mountains, the kind of accent they still had in the sort of places across America that didn't listen much to the radio or make it to the movies.

Cole's eyes were his most striking feature. They were nearly colorless, empty of any emotion. Spooky. The lieutenant looked away.

They headed back to headquarters, Mulholland leading the way and Cole following along a couple of paces behind, off to one side.

He found the other men waiting for him. There were three of them. With himself, Cole and the

French guide, that made six of them to take on the Jerries.

"Listen up, I'm Lieutenant Mulholland. I don't know how much you know, but basically we've been designated as a counter-sniper unit."

"Just six of us, sir?" asked a big, raw-boned soldier.

"That's right, soldier, just us." Mulholland knew it was crazy, one of those FUBAR situations that seemed an everyday occurrence in the United States Army. He couldn't tell that to these men, of course, so he put it in simpler terms. "The German snipers have been chewing us up something terrible, and it's our job to put a stop to it. What's your name, soldier?"

"Meacham, sir. Tom Meacham."

Meacham was some sort of farm boy, well over six feet tall. The rifle looked small in his hands. If they had been picking a football team, Meacham would have been his first choice. But a sniper? The kid looked like he'd be too big and clumsy.

"Do you have any experience as a sniper, Meacham?"

"I used to do some hunting back home," the kid said, managing to look embarrassed as he said it, like he'd been caught bragging.

Mulholland liked him and felt he could trust him.

He moved on to the next soldier. He had an olive complexion and a smirk. "Who are you, soldier?"

"Vaccaro, sir."

"What's your experience as a sniper, Vaccaro?

"I'm the best shot here. I've been on this beach for twenty-four hours and I've already sniped a dozen Jerries. I shot their Nazi asses off! Hell, we ought to be able to put marks on our rifles like the aces do when they shoot down planes."

"We'll see about that, Vaccaro."

The lieutenant moved down the line to the third man. "You're up," he said. "What's your name, soldier?"

"John Kingfisher, sir."

"What is your experience as a sniper, Kingfisher?"

He shrugged. "I got volunteered."

"Well, you must be good with a rifle."

The soldier shrugged again. "To be honest, sir, the colonel was asking around for guys who could shoot, and my captain wanted to make the colonel happy, so he sent me because I'm part Cherokee."

"You can shoot, right?" Mulholland asked hopefully.

"Sure I can shoot, as much as you can, sir. But before I was in the Army, the most shooting I done was at the county fair, plinking tin ducks in the shooting gallery."

"I can guarantee this is going to be different from the shooting gallery at the county fair. Cherokee, huh? OK, Chief, you're stuck with us now.

Vaccaro pointed to Cole. "What about him. Who are you?"

"The name's Micajah Cole."

"What the hell kind of name is that? Micajah? Is that even American?"

"What the hell kind of name is Vaccaro?" Cole replied. "Sounds more dago than American to me."

"Huh? Is that supposed to be a joke?"

"Micajah was a prophet in the Old Testament," Meacham spoke up shyly. "He warns the Assyrians that they will be defeated for defying God. *Thy kingdom will be plowed as a field and thy capital shall become a barren ruin.*"

"Well, shit, there you go," Vaccaro said. "If it's in the Bible, that's good enough for me. But lookin' at that Confederate flag on his helmet, I'm gonna call him Reb. Or maybe Hillbilly."

"It doesn't matter what his name is, Vaccaro," Mulholland said. "What matters is that Cole here is good with a rifle. He did quite a bit of damage with it yesterday when we came ashore. He's a good man to have on our team."

"You're the boss, sir."

"You just keep that in mind, Vaccaro, and we'll get along fine," the lieutenant said. He gestured toward their guide, who was watching from several feet away. "The last person on our team is *Mademoiselle*

Molyneux. She's a French Resistance fighter, and she's agreed to guide us through the hedgerow country."

"Mmm, mmm. She can guide me through her French bushes anytime she likes," Vaccaro wise-cracked.

"Shut up, Vaccaro. Headquarters tells me Miss Molyneux is one of the best guides there is and we're lucky to have her. She will try to keep your sorry ass from being killed, because I've been assured the countryside here is thoroughly mined and booby trapped. Our job will be to go in there and eliminate as many German snipers as possible, because they are playing holy hell with our infantry units."

It was some team, Mulholland thought. They were supposed to start conquering the Third Reich with a farmer, an Indian, a smart ass city kid, a French girl, and a hillbilly. God help them.

"Before we head out, I want to assess everyone's skills as a sniper. I need to know what I'm dealing with here. We're going to do a little shooting. Follow me."

Mulholland took them to a relatively empty section of the beach. In the distance, a perimeter had been set up for captured Germans, who stood about singly or in small groups, watching the activity on the beach. No one paid much attention to Mulholland's small team of soldiers, but their female French guide did get some notice. Her arrival was met with a few catcalls and whistles.

Using the heights as a backdrop, the lieutenant took a few empty booze bottles—there was no shortage of those around the empty German fortifications—and set them up on a sandbag. They now had a natural target range.

"Farm boy, you go first," Mulholland said. "Three shots. Let's see how good you are."

Meacham had a head-down, *aw shucks* look as he stepped forward. There was something awkward and slow moving about the farm kid, but you had the feeling that there was a lot of strength in those shoulders.

"Look on the bright side," Vaccaro said. "If Meacham here misses or runs out of bullets, he can beat the hell out of them."

It was clear from the easy way that Meacham handled the rifle that he was familiar with weapons. He put the rifle to his shoulder and fired. A bottle shattered. He worked the bolt and fired again, then again. Three bottles were gone.

"That's some good shooting," the lieutenant said. "You must have been hell on the rabbits and woodchucks back home. You're next, Chief."

"One request, sir. I really don't like to be called Chief."

"You hit those three bottles and I'll call you anything you want."

"Yes, sir."

Chief surprised them by sitting down on the sand, working his arm through the sling, and propping his elbows on his knees in a classic shooting position right out of boot camp. "I've never even fired this rifle, you know."

"Just go ahead, Chief."

"Pretend they're cowboys, Chief, and you'll mow them bottles right down!" Vaccaro said.

"Shut up, Vaccaro."

They left the soldier alone and let him aim. Their French guide was standing off to one side, watching the show, and Mulholland caught his men giving her sidelong looks. It was clear that they wanted to impress her. No surprise there. As the colonel had said, she was a knockout. But there was also a tough and mysterious air about the young woman. She had been fighting the Germans a lot longer than any of them, that was for sure.

Chief fired and one of the bottles shattered. He took aim again. There was the sharp crack of the rifle, and instantly the bottle exploded.

"One more, Chief, and you win the Kewpie Doll!"

He took aim and fired, but the bottle remained standing.

"Damn!" he said. "Must have been the wind."

"It ain't the wind, Chief," Vaccaro said. "It's just that your ancestors were better with a bow and arrow."

"Screw you, Vaccaro. Let's see how you do."

Vaccaro strutted forward—there was really no other way to describe it—and took aim. He fired three times, but hit nothing.

"Are there bullets in your rifle?" Chief asked. "Or were those blanks?"

"Goddamn thing ain't sighted in. Not my fault."

"Let me see it a minute, Vaccaro," said Mulholland, stepping forward to take the rifle. He inspected the weapon, but could detect no obvious fault with it, though it was very possible that the telescopic sight needed adjustment. He put the scope to the eye and one of the bottles sprang closer. With the crosshairs settled just where the shoulder of the bottle began to fatten, he squeezed the trigger, and the bottle shattered.

"Maybe it's not the rifle," the lieutenant said, handing it back. "Cole, let's see you shoot."

"Yeah, let's see if the hillbilly here really knows how to use a rifle," Vaccaro said.

Cole walked to the spot where the three others had shot from. So far, he had been the quietest of the group, and the French guide eyed him with interest. He had a tough, competent look about him that reminded her of some of the Resistance fighters she knew. Cole raised the rifle and fired three times in rapid succession, but none of the bottles was touched.

Vaccaro laughed. "You can't shoot for shit, Hillbilly! You're as bad as I am."

Mulholland was surprised, but he didn't let it show. He had already seen what Cole could do with a rifle. "That's all right, Cole. Maybe today just isn't your day."

"Uh, sir?" Meacham pointed into the distance, toward the German POW camp. Three bodies lay sprawled on the beach, and several of the POWs as well as the guards were running around, trying to determine where the shots had come from.

"Holy shit," Vaccaro said. "Hillbilly shot them!"

Mulholland was stunned. "Private Cole, you can't do that!"

Cole spat. "A lot of men died on this beach. What's three more dead Germans? I reckon I'm just evening the score."

"Hillbilly, you are goddamn crazy," Vaccaro said.

Mulholland wasn't sure what to do. Technically, Cole had just murdered three prisoners of war.

"Your hillbilly is right," their guide spoke up. "The Germans killed many innocent people."

Mulholland was still undecided about how to react when the colonel picked that very moment to wander over from HQ. The lieutenant opened his mouth to say something about the prisoners, but the colonel spoke first. "If ya'll are done shootin' up empty bottles, do you think you could shoot some Germans?"

"Shit, sir, the hillbilly here just did that."

Vaccaro might have said more, but the lieutenant gave him a warning look. *That goddamn Vaccaro,* Mulholland thought. He couldn't hit the broad side of a barn, but he could sure shoot his mouth off.

"What?" the colonel looked confused.

Lieutenant Mulholland started to salute, then dropped his arm upon remembering what their guide had said. "Yes, sir. We'll move out right away."

CHAPTER EIGHT

TOWARD NIGHTFALL, when it was safer to move, Von Stenger slipped away from the bridge. If he stayed, it would only be a matter of time before the Americans pinpointed his position. As he knew well from Russia, a sniper who kept moving was one who stayed alive.

So he and the boy hiked toward the beach and the sound of fighting. They kept to the smaller paths through the bocage, which reduced their chances of running into any Allied forces. The two of them alone could move silently and slip off the road, into the brush, whenever the need arose.

"*Herr Hauptmann*, are we going to stop tonight?" the boy sounded so weary, and Von Stenger could hear how he dragged his feet.

"If you stop, I will shoot you."

That shut the boy up. Although Von Stenger was much older, years of hard campaigning had given him lean muscles and inured him to the discomforts of not stopping to sleep or eat. Around midnight they heard voices ahead in the darkness—German voices —and came across a small unit that was setting up a series of defensive fallbacks in the hedgerows. Von Stenger volunteered his services as a sniper, and the captain in charge gladly accepted, teaming him up with another pair of snipers.

"My name is Wulf," said the taller sniper, a Wehrmacht corporal who appeared to be in his early twenties. He nodded at the other man. "That's Schultz. You look old enough to be my father, Pops. Are you one of the reserve units that was sent in?"

In the darkness, Von Stenger knew the corporal could not see his rank. "No, I have been a sharp-shooter for a while now."

"You went through the sniper training school?"

"Yes, I was an instructor there," Von Stenger said. He lit a cigarette and the flickering flame illuminated the Knight's Cross he wore. "Then I was a sniper in Spain, Poland and Russia. And you?"

"This is my first time in combat ... sir."

Von Stenger quickly sized them up. Wulf had a tough, competent look about him. Schultz appeared more nervous and kept checking and rechecking his rifle.

"Remember your training, Corporal, and you will do fine," Von Stenger said. "There will be many Americans here by morning. The woods and fields will be crawling with them. That I can promise you."

The German plan was simple, yet highly effective, taking full advantage of the Norman terrain. The countryside was laid out like a patchwork quilt, with few roads, so that the dense hedgerows formed the seams of the imaginary quilt. It would be necessary for the Americans to move cross country. To do so, they would have to push from one field to the next. It was all a little like one of those old houses where one had to walk through an adjacent bedroom to get to the bath because the house hadn't been designed with hallways. The Germans intended to make the Allied forces pay dearly for each step and every inch of territory.

The fields ranged in size from five or ten acres to expanses of twenty or even fifty acres. There were generally just one or two gaps in the hedge to allow a farmer access to his crops or livestock in the field. With their valuable head start on the allies, the Germans had placed snipers or machine gunners to cover the entrances to the fields. The only way in or out was through their gun sights. In essence, nearly all of Normandy was now an elaborate trap. This particular field was one of the first in from the beach.

"Wulf, we are going to do some shooting at

daybreak tomorrow," Von Stenger said. "The Allies are going to come pouring through here, but they won't know what hit them."

The three German snipers prepared to hide themselves at the far end of the field, which had a crop of tall winter wheat, but made certain they had a clear view of the entrance. There was an exit for themselves, but Von Stenger had Fritz help cut brush so that they could create a camouflage gate. It would only be a matter of time before too many Allied troops had made it into the field, but when that happened, the Germans could escape through the gate ... then start the whole process over again in the next field over.

"Are you ready, Corporal Wulf?" Von Stenger asked.

The younger man licked his lips. "Indeed I am."

"Remember, nothing too fancy. Take the body shot rather than the head shot. We are trying for kills here, not misses. We need those bodies to stack up like cordwood."

All that was left to do now was wait for daylight.

COLE'S EYES flicked across the landscape, which changed abruptly as they moved away from the beach. Grass replaced the sand, woods superseded the dunes, and where there had been the constant surge of surf and machinery on the beach, there was now the rustle of leaves and birdsong. If it hadn't been for the distant gunfire, they could have been going for a walk through the woods and fields back home.

Cole felt more at ease here than he had in months. He always had been a loner, having grown up in the woods and the mountains. The cramped quarters of Army life were not to his liking. Privacy was nonexistent. There was not so much as a toilet stall to grab a few minutes alone.

These weeks and even months of constantly crowded conditions had grated on Cole's nerves, though he was the kind of man who built a sort of armor or shell around himself. Other men sensed his solitary nature and left him alone.

In the quiet and solitude of the French country-side, his senses slowly came alive again, tingling awake like a cramped limb that had fallen asleep in the night. He heard birds, the sigh of the wind in the trees and the whisper of it on the grass. The air smelled of rain and wet earth. The country sounds and smells made Cole feel like he was home. A part of himself he had forgotten about stirred and came alive.

"This ain't so bad, is it, Lieutenant," Vaccaro said. He sounded too loud for the hushed countryside.

Vaccaro had a city voice. "We could be going up against Panzers. Those are the real bad asses. We just need to find a few stray Jerries with rifles."

"We'll see," Mulholland said. "Just keep your eyes open and pay attention."

"It's spooky quiet here," Chief said.

"Yeah," Mulholland agreed. "Listen, I want everyone to spread out. Keep twenty paces between you and the man in front of you. If a machine gun opens up on us, we don't want Jerry to take us all out in one burst."

"Does that apply to me as well, *mon lieutenant*?" asked Jolie, who was walking nearby.

"You bet," he said. "But you know this country. Don't you want to be first and lead the way?"

"*Non*, I do not," Jolie said. "The first person is more likely to step on a land mine."

"These roads are mined?" Mulholland asked, looking at the muddy road beneath his feet with fresh concern.

"It is hard to know for certain. The Germans did bury thousands of mines. Who knows where? Better not to go first." She nodded at Vaccaro. "Send that one first. He is useless but for a big mouth."

"Hey, sweetheart, I love you too."

"Shut up and pay attention, Vaccaro," Mulholland said. He remained at the head of the squad.

Cole was bringing up the rear, which was fine with

him. One by one, he sized up the members of their patrol. Meacham was twenty paces ahead of him, scanning the woods and fields with the eye of a country boy. He seemed all right.

Then came the Chief and Vaccaro. The Chief paid attention and seemed like a quick learner. Cole thought he would be a decent sniper—if he lived long enough.

Vaccaro might get them all killed on account of his loud mouth alone.

The lieutenant was a decent officer—he sure as hell had been brave enough on the beach yesterday, taking chances that Cole himself wouldn't have, if the lieutenant hadn't been leading the way. Mulholland was all right for an officer.

The French girl trailed a few paces behind the lieutenant. Cole was puzzled by the fact that she didn't seem particularly excited or grateful that they had come to liberate her country. She had a hardness to her, like a soup bone with all the meat boiled off. No nonsense. She also didn't talk too much, which was a quality Cole admired in a woman.

He pushed thoughts about his companions aside and kept his eyes moving, looking as far ahead as possible. The hedgerow country was unlike anything he had seen before. These hedgerows were ancient, going back to Roman times. They had begun as simple berms of earth to separate fields in order to corral livestock and define ownership. Over the centuries, brush and trees had grown on top of the earthen berms to form thick, almost impenetrable walls of greenery.

The hedgerows covered most of the Cotentin Peninsula as completely as a quilt across an old double bed. Unpaved lanes and roads passed through the bocage, some of these so thickly overhung with greenery that going down the road was like passing through a tunnel. After dark, the bocage would have been the perfect setting for a werewolf story.

But in this nightmare world, there were no werewolves or vampires. Snipers were far more real and deadly. This living maze was perfect for defensive action such as that now being undertaken by the Germans as they worked to thwart the Allied advance. Worse yet for the Americans was the fact that the few points of high ground scattered around the bocage offered an excellent vantage point. A German sniper on one of these hill tops could look down into the fields and lanes—and pick off anything that moved. In the hours after D-Day, nearly all this high ground had been occupied by German troops moving into defensive positions.

Their squad had orders to engage the enemy. But first, they had to find them. Cole suspected that the French countryside would not be quiet for long.

After the French woman's remark about the

Germans mining the roads, most of the others kept looking down at the dirt and grass, expecting to see some hint of a mine, but Cole reminded himself that he needed to look up for the real danger, which happened to be German troops, snipers, and Panzers.

"This is where we leave the road," Jolie said. "The road here will just take us in a circle. It is necessary to have to use a map and compass from this point on."

Lieutenant Mulholland followed Jolie's suggestion and led them toward a gap in a hedgerow into an expanse of field, newly green with spring. They entered the field only after Lieutenant Mulholland and Meacham had advanced some distance into it. The field encompassed perhaps twenty acres and was ringed by the green-walled hedgerow, which managed to give the field the feel of a sprawling football field surrounded by bleachers.

On the opposite side of the field was a similar gap that Cole figured led to the next field over. A squad of American soldiers was crouched on either side of the gap. He could see two bodies sprawled in the grass just inside the neighboring field.

They moved around to the edge of the field, keeping out of any line of fire offered by the gap, then approached the other squad. Mulholland got together with the squad leader. Though their voices were low, Cole was close enough to hear the two offi-cers talking.

"We've got orders to clear this field, but German snipers have got the gap covered," the captain said. "They've already shot two of my men. I just wish we had a goddamn Sherman tank with us—we could follow along behind it. But we don't have one, so thank God you all came along."

"Us?"

"You're counter snipers, right? You've all got telescope sights on your rifles. Fight fire with fire, I always say. This is your operation now, Lieutenant."

"Yes, sir," Mulholland said uncertainly. "How many Germans are there?"

"We're pretty sure there are three because the shots are coming from different directions."

"Where are they located?"

"Damned if I know. Walk into that field and you'll find out, Lieutenant." The captain slumped back against a large stone and lit a cigarette. "Hell, if this is what we have facing us between here and Paris, it's going to make the beach landing yesterday look like a kindergarten birthday party. Where did you all come ashore?"

"Omaha."

The captain dragged on his cigarette. "We were at Utah, thank God. I heard what you went through. Sounds like a goddamn nightmare."

The captain spoke loud enough for them all to hear, and Cole's thoughts went back to poor Jimmy, shot on the beach. It sure was a long way to go from home just to get killed by the Germans. Cole didn't really understand what Hitler or the Germans wanted, but he understood the empty stare in Jimmy's dead eyes.

"So what's your plan here?" the captain asked.

The lieutenant was taking a while to answer, so Cole spoke up. "I reckon I might have an idea, sir," he said.

"All right, Cole. It's got to be better than the plan I've got right now, which is nothing."

"Let me bring two men through that gap to draw the snipers' fire, and you can locate their position and take them out."

"Sounds like a good way to get three men killed."

"We'll split up and run in different directions. The way I figure it, the Germans will probably miss. It's hard to hit a running target. Three running targets is confusing. But when they fire, they'll reveal their positions. We'll have our boys at the edges of the gap to take them out."

"Hell, Cole, the only one here who's good enough to do that is you."

"Meacham is a good shot. Chief can at least make them keep their heads down."

The lieutenant thought it over. It wasn't much of a plan, but it was better than nothing. "Take Vaccaro with you," he said quietly. "With any luck, he can run as fast as he can run his mouth. The captain here will have to volunteer one of his men to come with me."

"One more thing," Cole said. "I need me a ball of twine."

It took a couple of minutes to organize the attack. The twine was normally used for marking off landing zones and trenches, but Cole had another idea. Meacham slid along the grass to take up a position so that his rifle just peeked out from the edge of the gap. His field of fire was limited by the tall June grass, but the grass in turn hid him from the enemy snipers already in position. He would just have to be lucky and get a clear shot.

Chief would cross the gap and take up position on the other side once Cole started running. Nobody could pass in front of the gap now because the snipers had it covered.

Cole and Vaccaro stripped off their packs and prepared to run like hell through the gap, into the field, toward the enemy snipers. They were joined by a kid from the other squad who had the build of a rabbit.

"Hillbilly, you are about to get us killed," Vaccaro said.

"When you get in that field, you two run like hell and zigzag to make a poor target. Run at an angle if you can, not right toward them. Whatever you do, don't bunch up." He tied the end of a piece of twine to a stick that was about two feet long and handed it to the rabbit-looking kid. The rest of the twine was wound lightly in Cole's utility pocket so that it would unwind as they ran.

"What's the stick for?" the kid asked.

"That there's our decoy. Now, you look like you can run fast. If I was you, I'd run like there was hornets after you. I want you to drop that stick about halfway across."

On the face of it, running into the field in front of the German snipers seemed crazy and foolish. But the key was to split up. Once, when hunting high up in the hills, Cole had startled a pack of coyotes feeding at a deer kill. He had raised his rifle to shoot one, anticipating that they would flee in one direction, when the coyotes did a curious thing. They split into three or four different directions. He'd been so surprised that he hadn't got off a good shot at any of the coyotes. They all got away.

Also, he knew it was considerably harder to hit a running target than a stationary one. If the Germans had been using a machine gun, he and the other two runners would be killed in a single burst of automatic fire. But a man with a rifle had to pick a target, lead it, and fire.

Not so easy to do.

Cole used to practice on old truck tires that his sister would roll downhill with a paper target strung up in the middle. It was hard enough to hit a rolling tire, let alone a zigzagging, running man.

He was sure the Germans wouldn't be much better at it than he was. His life was counting on it.

Cole took a deep breath. His heart pounded.

"Go!" he shouted.

CHAPTER NINE

VON STENGER WAS WATCHING the gap through the telescopic sight, which narrowed his field of vision significantly, but enabled him to keep a close eye on any effort by the American troops to break through. He knew, with satisfaction, that three bodies already lay in the field. Corporal Wulf, who was somewhere to his left, had shot one. Von Stenger had shot the other two. The third sniper, Schultz, would get his turn soon enough. They had the Allied advance into this field pinned down—at least for now.

There. Three men came sprinting through the gap in the hedgerow. All at once they ran in three different directions. Von Stenger was taken by surprise, and the men ran so quickly that he lost track of them in the scope's limited field of vision. One's eyes could sometimes notice small details faster than the brain could process them, and that is what happened now. He saw that two of the three carried rifles with telescopic sights. Snipers.

The one farthest back had some kind of flag painted on his helmet. He had to pull the rifle away from his eye long enough to acquire the targets again. He then used the hunter's trick of keeping his gaze on the runners as he raised the telescopic sight to his eye, thus keeping them in view.

One of the runners turned left and he heard Wulf's rifle fire on this left, and then Schultz fired once, twice, three times. Stupid. Making himself a target. Then someone fired from the direction of the gap and Schultz's rifle fell silent.

He couldn't think about that now as he tracked the two remaining runners. The first one was a smallish man who dodged and twisted like the world's fastest drunk. In an instant, the crosshairs lined up on the chest and Von Stenger blew his heart out. He moved his shoulder and chin slightly as he readjusted his aim to take the other runner, who should be slightly to the right.

But the man was nowhere to be seen. At more than a foot tall, the late spring grass was just high enough to hide someone. He scanned the grass, looking for movement. Something twitched in the grass. Von Stenger did not have a clear target, but he fired anyhow, trusting to luck.

In response, a bullet flicked past his ear, so close that it made every nerve of his body tingle and quiver. His first reaction was to roll or move, but he forced himself to stay still. He was certain the shot had not come from the other side of the field, but from the tall grass. The second American sniper was still out there. Had the man seen him, or like Von Stenger, had he simply made his best guess at the target? If the American sniper had simply missed, he would shoot again. He braced himself for a second shot. When it did not come, he thought *don't move*.

"Herr Hauptmann?" Fritz had crawled up behind him. "The Americans will be coming."

"Keep still." Von Stenger exhaled the words more than saying them. "Do not move a muscle."

He kept his eye pressed to the sight, hoping for some movement in the grass, which swayed gently in the breeze. He felt a stirring of excitement he had not felt in a while, not since Russia, when he had faced a particularly cunning enemy sniper and taken a bullet through his leg as a result. The wound was serious enough to get him flown back to Berlin to recuperate.

That wound had saved his life. Not long after that the Russian noose had tightened and evacuations ended. Legions of poor Wehrmacht bastards had been left behind to starve or freeze.

He sometimes wondered what had become of the

Russian who shot him. The Russian liked to leave behind playing cards—a rather flashy trait for a Soviet sniper. Had he been one of the famous ones? Or just some lucky peasant?

Von Stenger liked a clever opponent. A sniper duel was much like a deadly game of chess. Von Stenger had boxed in his youth and taken part in vicious, if foolish, fencing matches at the military academy that left him with a jauntily scarred face, but this was the most exciting game there was. If he moved, the American might shoot him. If he did not move, the American might shoot him. Checkmate. But if the American made some movement in the grass, it would be as bad as exposing his own king piece.

He played back in his mind how the men had run into the field. Only two were carrying sniper rifles. The man Von Stenger had shot had been running ahead with an open sight M1. A decoy then. A pawn. Could the American sniper really be as ruthless as that? Not even Russians were that bad. Or should he say, that good.

Then the chess board changed abruptly. The American squad came pouring through the gap in the hedge. From the field behind Von Stenger a barrage of Wehrmacht mortars came rolling in. They were firing blind, but it was enough to send the Americans scrambling for cover.

He waited until two more mortar rounds thumped down in the field, then quickly rolled to the left and scooted backwards like a crab until he was down the other side of the thick, ancient wall inside the hedgerow. Briars clawed at his face and the trunks of scrawny trees and saplings grew so close together it was almost like being in a cage. Crawling, Von Stenger could just get through the dense underbrush.

"Come on," he said to the boy.

"*Herr Hauptmann*, what about Wulf and Schultz?"

"They will catch up if they are not dead," Von Stenger said. "Now bring my gear along. We are going hunting."

* * *

"Good God almighty," Meacham said. It was as close as he could come to swearing. He was trembling, white faced, on the edge of shock. "I just killed a man."

"That was some fine shooting," Lieutenant Mulholland said.

"I really killed that German."

"Killed the hell out of him," Vaccaro agreed.

They were looking down at the dead body of a German private. Meacham had fired from the gap in the hedge when the German sniper opened up on Cole and the others running across the field.

Meacham's bullet had caught the sniper in the cheek-bone, killing him instantly. The dead man's hands still grasped the Mauser with its telescopic sight.

Meacham was looking very pale, so Mulholland grabbed him by the shoulders and shook him hard, the way a coach might get a player to get his head back in the game. "This is a war, Meacham. You were doing your duty. You got him, so he didn't get you or anybody else. Good work."

Cole hadn't gotten his German. The mortars coming down in the field had given the other sniper cover to slip away. Cole was fairly certain that if he'd gotten some hint of movement from the sniper, then he would have been able to hit him. No such luck. The German had evaporated like the morning mist.

When the mortars stopped, the squad moved across the field and Cole worked his way back into the hedgerow until he found the spot the German had been using as a sniper's nest. He spotted the stub of a fancy French cigarette, bright white against the leaf mold, along with the bright brass wink of several empty shell casings. He picked one up and realized that it was not German. They had seen plenty of Mauser casings strewn around the beach fortifications, but none like this.

He bent closer to the earth and found boot prints. He touched them, wondering at the fact that the man he'd been trying to kill—and who had tried to kill him—had made them just minutes before. He guessed the man was somewhere from average height to maybe six feet tall, probably 180 pounds. Farther back he found a different set of boot prints. They were about the same size, but they were made by the cheaper hobnail boots issued to German enlisted men, and these didn't go as deep into the soil, so it was a lighter man. Maybe a spotter? He understood that the German snipers often worked in teams.

Both sets of boot prints showed where the two men had scrambled and slid down the far side of the ancient wall at the center of the hedge. Clearly, they had gone into the next field, but Cole could glimpse nothing through the thick brush.

He worked his way back out of the hedge and rejoined the other men in the squad.

Meacham still looked pale, while Vaccaro glared at him as he walked up. "Hillbilly, your trick with that stick actually worked."

"I tugged at the string to make the stick move in the grass so the sniper would shoot at it and give himself away."

"Holy shit, Hillbilly, you are one backwards son of a bitch," Vaccaro said, but with something like admiration in his voice. "We've got Sherman tanks and bazookas, and you're fighting the Nazis with sticks and string. The question is, did it work?"

Cole shrugged. "Well, he fired, all right, but I

didn't have a clear shot and I missed. He left a few of these behind."

Cole held out the brass he'd found in the German sniper's nest. Lieutenant Mulholland took it, looked at the markings that read 7.62 Л П С г ж and announced, "That's Cyrillic writing on the casing. I don't know what it says, but it's Russian ammunition. He must be shooting a Mosin Nagant, which is a Russian sniper rifle. I don't know why."

"I've heard it's a better rifle. Sturdier and more accurate than the Mauser," Cole said. He thought about that. "The only way to get one would be if you served in Russia."

"How the hell could some German take away a Russian sniper's rifle?" Vaccaro wanted to know.

"By shooting him," Cole said.

CHAPTER TEN

THE NEXT FIELD was held by German machine gunners that had dug themselves in like ticks, eager for blood and just as hard to remove. The squad that the snipers had met up with went in first and got halfway across the field when the German gunner opened up, chewing several GIs into raw meat. The rest found themselves pinned down, unable to move as bullets whipped overhead.

"It's a goddamn slaughter," Mulholland announced, watching in horror through a gap in the hedge as one soldier tried to rush the Germans and was nearly cut in half by a burst. "If we don't do something, the next squad through here is going to walk into the same trap."

Cole had the solution. He crawled back into the hedgerow to where the German sniper had been and followed his tracks down into the killing field. From there, it was hard to tell where the sniper had gone, but he could see the German machine gunners at work from his concealed position.

He heard a noise behind him and spun, crouching low and pulling his .45 at the same time, but it was only the French girl following him.

"What are you doing?" he snapped, annoyed.

"Same as you," she said. "Killing Germans."

She carried a battered old rifle that looked as likely to blow up in her face as shoot straight, but Cole supposed that was the best that the French Resistance could get. It reminded him a lot of some old mountain rifle from back home. He looked the rifle over doubtfully, but liked the determined expression on her face. It was her country, after all, so as far as he was concerned she could have at it if she wanted to snipe at the Jerries with that antique. He nodded, and they crept out of the hedge together.

The machine gunners were busy shooting up the squad and they didn't notice Cole hunkered at the edge of the field. He got the German gunner's helmet in his sights and punched a bullet through the steel. Another man grabbed for the machine gun, and Cole shot him as well. He was about to shoot the third man reaching for the handles on the machine gun when something went bang off to his right. He'd damn near forgotten the French girl.

Her bullet only kicked up dirt at the edge of the German foxhole, which got the machine gunner's attention. He swiveled the weapon in their direction and the black hole of the machine gun's muzzle looked as big as the moon through Cole's rifle sight. He let his breath out, fired, and nailed the German before he could depress the trigger on the machine gun.

"That was my target," he muttered.

"You shoot too slow," she said.

"At least I hit what I shoot at."

What was left of the American squad out in the middle of the field got up and dusted themselves off. Several torn, bloody bodies lay scattered in the grass where the German machine gunners had caught them.

"So far we've captured two fields and lost maybe ten men," Cole said. "This war ain't goin' so well, if you ask me."

"Americans have no stomach for a fight," Jolie said. "Where is your anger at the enemy? You do not know how to hold a grudge."

For the first time since leaving the English coast, Cole laughed. "Darlin', you don't know the half of it. My people back home invented that there word. We got grudges against other families, we got grudges against Yankees, we got grudges against the government. And right about now, I got a serious grudge against Germans."

"Then let us go shoot some more," Jolie said.

"Keep talkin' like that and you're goin' to get me all hot and bothered, missy."

Jolie snorted like a horse, which Cole thought wasn't very French lady like, but he followed along as they headed back to join up with the other snipers. They hadn't been able to do much good in the last firefight, but at least Meacham had recovered somewhat and didn't look so pale.

They crossed the field and went through a gap in the hedge that opened onto a narrow dirt road. A large American squad was moving along it in the distance, and at the head of the unit Cole could see a Sherman tank. It was the first one he had seen in action away from the beach, but he wasn't sure how much good it could do out here. The hedges were so dense and the openings between fields were so tight that tanks were confined to the country roads, which were heavily mined. In addition, German squads armed with anti-tank rockets lay in wait.

To make matters worse for the tanks, somewhere out there were heavily armored German Tiger tanks, which would be more than a match for the Sherman tanks. Above the distant rumble of the tank engine, Cole could hear the rattle of small arms fire and the heavier thump of artillery. Somebody was catching hell somewhere.

"Miss Molyneux, where does this road go?" Lieutenant Mulholland wanted to know.

"We are moving toward St. Lo," Jolie said. "But this road does not go there directly."

"Well, it's a start," Mulholland said. "We're going to stay on this road until called upon to deploy against German snipers."

"Lieutenant, we should let that tank up there deploy against snipers," Vaccaro said. "Looks to me like it's bulletproof."

"Wouldn't do much good," the lieutenant said. "It would be like using a sledgehammer to drive a nail, when what you need is a hammer. And we're the hammer."

"Last time I got hammered, I managed to nail a sweet little English girl," Vaccaro said. "That's the kind of hammering and nailing I like to do."

They all laughed at that, harder than they should have, and Chief cracked a joke about the girl costing Vaccaro not one but two cartons of cigarettes, which got them laughing harder.

They started to feel the tense mood that had come over them lift. It was funny, in a war, how you could go from being scared to death to being giddy about the simple fact of being alive, all in the space of a morning.

Their laughter was cut short, however, when they came around a bend in the narrow road and saw a handful of American troops at the side of the road, gathered around a German on his knees, with his hands raised in surrender. An American sergeant had a pistol out and it was pointed at the German's head. He lowered the .45 when he caught sight of the approaching sniper squad.

The German was youthful and blond-haired, but he was clearly in pain. His coat was off, revealing a gray undershirt crisscrossed with suspenders, and there was a deep red stain on his side where he had been wounded. It was obvious as well from the fresh bruises and cuts on his face that he had been roughed up. Next to the soldier's coat and helmet was a Mauser with a telescopic sight.

"What's going on here?" Mulholland asked.

"Best just move along, sir," the sergeant said. "We have this under control."

"I demand to know what's going on, Sergeant. That's an order!"

The sergeant seemed to think it over. He was an older man, not some kid, with heavy stubble not quite obscuring the lines of exhaustion etched on his face. In civilian life he might have been a shop fore-man, the kind of man used to some authority. There didn't seem to be any officers around.

"He's a sniper," the sergeant said. "He shot three of our guys trying to cross a field before we winged him."

"You know the rules, Sergeant. Captured Germans get sent to the rear."

"Not this one. Not a sniper. They're killers and murderers, sir, not regular soldiers." For the first time, the sergeant seemed to notice that the lieutenant's squad was armed with rifles that had telescopic sights. "I'm not saying that about our own men, mind you. But these are the goddamn Krauts we're talking about."

"I'm not so sure the Germans wouldn't feel the same way about us," Mulholland said.

"That's a chance we all take, ain't it, sir? Now, let me say it one more time. It's best if you just move along."

Almost imperceptibly, there seemed to be a change in the air. The squad of Americans gripped their weapons more tightly. There were at least twenty of them—and only six in their own sniper squad. Cole shifted his own weight and put a hand on his automatic. Beside him, Jolie glanced at him nervously. She had felt the tension, too. Cole looked around at the faces—exhausted, bloody, dirty—and it was clear to him that if it came down to it, these men would start shooting before they gave up their prisoner.

"Lieutenant, I reckon we ought to move out," Cole said.

"Sir, they're going to shoot him," Meacham said. "That's against all the Geneva Convention rules."

"Shut up, Farm Boy," Cole said. "You ain't helping any. Last time I heard we were at war with the Germans, and I reckon that means we're going to kill a few of them along the way. Sir?"

Mulholland didn't move or speak, so Cole got a good grip on the handle of the .45. Here he was about to get in a shootout with their own boys, but he reckoned there were stranger things that happened in a war. He was familiar with what happened when emotions ran high and everybody had guns.

"Let's move out," Mulholland finally said, his voice strained.

They continued down the road, leaving the squad surrounding the German. They hadn't gone far when there was a single pistol shot. Cole looked back and saw the German's body at the side of the road.

"That was messed up," Vaccaro said.

"It was wrong, just plain wrong," said Meacham.

"Sometimes it ain't about right or wrong," Cole said. "It's about gettin' even."

"Do you think the Germans would do that to us if we got captured?" Vaccaro asked.

"Probably," Cole said. "But the upside of that is your chances of gettin' killed first are pretty good."

"You know how to cheer a guy up, Hillbilly. Lieutenant, what do you think?"

"I think you should shut the hell up, Vaccaro. You talk too much."

After that, the lieutenant quickened his pace and walked several steps in front of them.

"Ya'll spread out," Cole said.

"Who made you boss, Hillbilly?" Vaccaro demanded.

"You want to get shot, come up here and put your arm around my shoulders so we make a better target."

"Aw, go fuck your sister," Vaccaro said, but he took the hint and dropped back several paces.

The rest of the squad did the same. Lieutenant Mulholland was at the front, followed by Chief, then Cole and the others, all strung out now along the road like prayer beads. Jolie walked a few paces behind Cole.

The road passed between the hedges, which created a thick wall on either side. It reminded Cole a bit too much of a cattle chute. He felt exposed and would be glad to get back into the fields, but the lieutenant seemed intent on following this road.

The squad led by the Sherman tank was just visible in the distance, moving toward a gentle hill presided over by a stone church steeple. One of the things Cole had noticed about France was all the old buildings seemed to be built of stone or brick, while back home even the oldest churches and houses were mostly clapboard. The farms here had been built to last—hell, some of the stone barns in Normandy must be centuries old. The whole countryside dripped with history.

Coming across the execution of the German sniper had cast a pall over them. It was one thing to kill the enemy when he was shooting back, but quite another to shoot a man who had his hands up in the air. Who had surrendered to you. It didn't sit right with them. Cole had known there wasn't a thing they could do to stop it, but the execution still nagged at him. He realized that he himself had gone down a similar road since landing on the beach yesterday morning. He had shot those prisoners in the distance out of spite—mostly to show off. And also because he'd gone a little crazy, a little off the rails. He could understand that now.

Killing someone up close was different—harder and colder, somehow. What he had done wasn't right, but it hadn't felt wrong, either. Well, it was something to think about, which way a man wanted to be in a war. Would you be like a wild dog and kill just to kill, or more like a wolf—a predator that only hunted when it needed to, but that was feared nonetheless.

* * *

VON STENGER WAS AMAZED by the view from the church steeple. He could literally see for miles—the long stretch of fields reaching toward the sea to the east, and more countryside dotted with farms and villages all the way to St. Lo. The signs of war were everywhere by now as columns of Allied troops encountered stubborn knots of German resistance. Smoke. Churned earth. Bodies. If only he could have stayed up in the tower, there was no telling how much good he could have done. Targets presented themselves endlessly.

He had been watching for one group in particular, the snipers he had tangled with back in the field. A lucky shot by the Americans had done for Private Schultz, ending his brief career as a sniper, but Von Stenger and Wulf had slipped away with Fritz.

Wulf was stationed at a window in the stairway landing about halfway up. The next-to-useless boy Fritz was downstairs, guarding the entrance to the tower. The thought did not give Von Stenger much confidence, but at least the boy would be able to see the enemy approaching. With any luck, he might fire a few shots that would serve as a warning to Von Stenger and Wulf.

On the road that led toward the sea, Von Stenger caught sight of the group of American snipers who had given him so much trouble. *Hallo, alte Freunde. Hello, old friends.* He let the crosshairs sweep over them. He picked out the lieutenant leading them as well as the sniper with the flag on his helmet.

Von Stenger was a sufficient student of military history to recognize the flag as a symbol of the Confederate States of America. This sniper would be an American Southerner. He would be tough and resourceful, maybe even a bit of an outlaw. He remembered that the Confederates were called Rebels. Von Stenger was sure this was the man who had outsmarted him back in that field. That was all right. He liked a challenge.

So far, none of the American snipers had bothered with camouflage. More babes in the woods, he thought. There appeared to be a woman with them, which took Von Stenger by surprise. She wore civilian clothes. French Resistance? Well, well. Perhaps the local Gestapo had been too lenient in eliminating the Reich's enemies. They should have shot a few more Frenchmen—and women—to get the message across.

The tank coming up the road was worrisome. He could tell at a glance that it was no Tiger tank, being much smaller, but it was a threat nonetheless if the Americans opted to open fire on the tower. Behind the tank came what appeared to be a company of infantry, plodding along in the clanking wake of their armored companion.

So many targets, he thought. Where to begin? Von Stenger let the crosshairs float back to the French woman, and then to the sniper with the flag on his helmet. Not yet. His thoughts drifted to

Goethe: "It is not doing the thing we like to do, but liking the thing we have to do, that makes life blessed."

He settled the crosshairs on the sniper behind them and squeezed off a shot.

CHAPTER ELEVEN

COLE LOOKED BACK to ask Jolie a question and at that moment something zipped past his ear. A split second later he heard the distant crack of a rifle shot.

"Take cover!" the lieutenant shouted, but there wasn't anywhere to go. Cole felt a little like he had when Norma Jean Elwood caught him skinny dipping in Hog Creek and stole his clothes off the bank. The difference was that Norma Jean was trying to embarrass him, not kill him. He got in close to the hedge and hoped the brush would break up the line of fire. Jolie was right beside him.

Chief wasn't fast enough getting off the road. The next bullet hit him square in the chest. He had a look of surprise on his face. Chief staggered. Then he sank to his knees in the middle of the dirt road.

"Chief!" Cole ran to him, stooped down, and got

one of Chief's arms across his shoulders. He half dragged, half carried him toward the hedge, but Chief was heavy as hell weighted down with all his gear. Chief's own legs weren't moving. Dead weight, thought Cole. Jolie ran out and grabbed Chief's other arm, and they managed to get him to the hedge, out of sight of the sniper.

Cole shook him. "Chief? Chief?"

But there was no answer. The eyes stared blankly ahead. Looking more closely, Cole could see why— the bullet had struck him in the heart. A 7.62 mm rifle round traveling at thousands of feet per second built up an awful lot of what the Army trainers called kinetic energy. Cole would have described it as being kicked by a mule. Chief never had a chance.

"Mon dieu," Jolie said gently, then reached over and closed Chief's eyelids. "He is gone."

There was only one vantage point from which the sniper could have fired. The church steeple. Even so, the steeple was nearly half a mile away. To hit someone in the chest from that distance was goddamn impressive, to say the least. Cole wondered if he could have done that.

Surely, just for a moment, he had been in the sniper's sights. The thought made his skin crawl.

Lieutenant Mulholland crept along the hedge, out of view of the church steeple, until he reached Cole. "Chief?"

Cole shook his head. "Shot through the heart."

"That goddamn sniper is in the tower."

"I know."

"We're going to get him," Mulholland said. "If we don't, he can shoot up all the woods and fields around here for as far as he can see."

"All right then," Cole said. His eyes, which looked like they could have been made of cut glass, were so devoid of emotion that they startled the lieutenant. "Let's go kill us a sniper."

There was nothing they could do with Chief's body but leave it, so they moved it as far off the road as they could so that it wouldn't get run over by tanks or Jeeps. Lieutenant Mulholland bowed his head and said a prayer, and then in the shelter of the hedgerow, the five of them continued along the road. But now the sniper was busy picking off soldiers in the squad ahead of them. Those soldiers were packed more tightly in the road and had nowhere to go to get out of the line of fire. The sniper was having a field day with them, firing steadily at the crowded troops.

"Like shooting possums in a barrel," Cole muttered.

"I think you mean fish in a barrel," Vaccaro said.

"I've shot possums, whereas what kind of jackass shoots fish?" Cole said. "Back home, the best way to go fishin' is with dynamite."

"That ain't normal, Hillbilly. Is that what you do for entertainment back there in the hills? The rest of the world just goes to see a movie or maybe a baseball game."

"Will you both shut up please," Jolie said in her heavily accented English. "We must stop this German."

But the Sherman tank was already doing a good job of that. Located at the head of the column, the tank was taking aim at the top of the church steeple. The shells hadn't been all that accurate, but the scream of the passing rounds must have scared the hell out of the sniper up there taking aim at the soldiers. So far, he hadn't abandoned his post. His shots, fired at steady intervals, continued to chip away at the American ranks like so many hatchet blows.

Then the Sherman fired again, blowing a chunk out of the church steeple. A tremendous cheer went up from the troops. However, the old stone steeple seemed to dust itself off and remained standing tall. Then the sniper up there fired again, killing a man standing not far from the tank. Undeterred and impervious to the rifle rounds, the swift-moving Sherman roared up the road, closer to the steeple. Five or six soldiers clung to the outside, hanging on for dear life to whatever handles and footholds they could find. Once the tank carried them close enough, they could rush the base of the steeple and put an end to the sniper.

The Sherman tank had been chosen personally by General Patton for its speed and agility. The tank also had advantages in that it could be transported by rail car. Shermans were small and light enough that it was possible to land them on the beaches of Normandy. But it soon became clear that in almost every way that mattered in combat, the Sherman had revealed itself as an inferior adversary.

The Sherman had three major drawbacks that became apparent as soon as they began to engage enemy tanks in combat. The first issue was that the turret-mounted cannon was too small. Rounds from the Sherman literally bounced off the German tanks. Second, the armor plating was much too light and enemy anti-tank rounds went through them like a hot knife through butter. A single hit turned the Sherman tanks into fireballs, quickly earning them the nickname "Tommy Cookers" among Panzer units.

But at the moment, the Sherman was doing a good job of thwarting the sniper in the church steeple.

"Looks like that tank is going to do our job for us," said Lieutenant Mulholland as they double timed it up the road.

Just as quickly, the tables turned. From a patch of woods beside the church appeared a beast of a tank painted in blue-gray hues. It was one of the dreaded Tiger tanks. Bigger, heavily armored, and with a more powerful 88 mm cannon, it was more than a match for the American Sherman tank.

"Holy shit!" cried Vaccaro. "Look at that goddamn monster!"

Still, the Sherman moved gamely ahead, stopping to let off the men who had hitched a ride. They ran for cover as the Sherman quickly adjusted its range and fired, hitting the Tiger dead on. But when the burst cleared, there was no more damage to the Tiger tank than a scorch mark. The Sherman fired again, and this time the troops could hear the *karoom* of the shell ricocheting off the German tank.

The Tiger appeared to be taking its time. The gun raised a bit with an audible whirring of gears, and then the tank fired, sending out a shockwave of flame. The shell hit the Sherman dead on and the tank shuddered. After a few seconds, the hatch opened and a man started to climb out, black smoke pouring from the interior of the tank like smoke from a chimney. A shot rang out from the church steeple, and the tank crewman slumped in the hatchway. The smoke thickened and was soon followed by a lick of flame. Seconds later came a *whump* and a fireball as the gasoline exploded. The Sherman had lived up to its German nickname.

At an almost leisurely pace, the Tiger tank

advanced toward the American troops. Without their short-lived protector, they were helpless as the Tiger opened up with its machine gun. The men who had been advancing toward the church steeple had no choice but to fall back.

"Lieutenant, what should we do?" Meacham wanted to know.

"Run!"

There was nowhere to go but back down the road the way they had come. The Tiger was able to push past the burning hulk of the Sherman tank and get onto the road, causing panic among the American forces. The thick hedges on either side of the road kept them hemmed in and there was no time to force their way through—not with a Tiger tank hot on their trail. All the while the machine gun continued to chatter, spewing death as the tank rolled down the road.

The Tiger's hatch flipped open and a German wearing goggles appeared. But there was no time to take a shot at him. Cole and the other snipers had no choice but to run like hell, hoping that they would come to a gap in the hedge before the Tiger tank got in range. Though not as fast as the Sherman, the Tiger was quickly gaining on them. Before long, the whir of the gears and clank of the treads was as loud as the machine gun, and Cole could smell exhaust fumes. He was about to be mowed down by the tank's machine gun—or become a permanent part of the French road thanks to the tank's brutal treads.

From the corner of his eye, he saw that Jolie had stumbled, and he reached out to take her by the elbow. "Come on!"

Bullets whistled past his ear. Damn! How far was it to the next gap in the hedge? It was their only hope.

Then a blast from behind threw them both to the road, their momentum leaving Cole and Jolie in a tangle of arms and legs.

He thought the tank had fired and was surprised to see that it was now a smoking ruin behind them— a little too close behind them.

Jolie stared in awe. "How is this possible?"

They looked up at the sound of someone cackling. To Cole, it sounded like insane laughter. There were a few larger trees making their way up through the hedges, and in one of these sat a British paratrooper straddling a limb with his feet dangling down, like he was riding a rail. He was holding the smoking, empty tube of an M1A1 bazooka.

"Got 'em, by God!" he yelled. "Sent 'em a present right down the rabbit hole, ha, ha!"

The soldier climbed down and kneeled with the bazooka over one shoulder, then nodded at a bazooka rocket propped up nearby. "I found this thing by the side of the road and thought I'd put it to good use.

Lend a hand, mate, and load me up. It's the least you can do, considering I just saved your Yankee arse."

Cole fed the shell into the rear of the tube, hooked the fuse wire to the launcher, and tapped the Brit on the shoulder.

"You best look out," Cole told him. "There's a sniper in the church steeple."

"Not anymore," the Brit said, and fired at the church. The top of the steeple exploded, spewing stone and smoke, and through it all came the sharp gong of the church bell. "Now that's how to make short work of a Jerry sniper."

Having tossed down the empty bazooka tube, the British soldier got to his feet. By now, the scattered sniper squad had regrouped. Meacham had been nicked in the leg by a machine gun bullet, and came up limping, but Lieutenant Mulholland and Vaccaro had made it through unscathed.

"Private James Neville, British Sixth Airborne Division," he said, shaking hands all the way around, as if they were at a pub, rather than in the middle of a road in war-torn Normandy. "What you'll find with your Tiger tanks is that they are tough as a nut to crack, except from above, which is where the Nazis made the armor plating thinner to save on weight. Hit 'em there and it's like a good, swift kick in the bollocks. Of course, it's even better if the Jerries have the top open, ha, ha!"

They gazed in wonder at the burning wreck of the Tiger. No one had come climbing out right after the tank was hit, and judging from the spreading flames, they wouldn't be getting out now.

"We were goners," Lieutenant Mulholland said. "We can't thank you enough."

"I think he got the sniper as well," Meacham said. "I haven't heard any more shots from the steeple."

"We'd better investigate," Lieutenant Mulholland said. "It's our job to eliminate snipers, and if he's not dead, we can't leave him in place to shoot the hell out of the next unit to come down this road."

"Mind if I tag along?" the Brit said.

"Suit yourself," the lieutenant said. "Where's your unit?"

"Scattered between the coast and Paris, I'd wager," Neville said. "The drop yesterday morning was something of a TARFU."

"What's that?" the lieutenant asked.

"Totally and Royally Fucked Up," Neville explained. "It's like your SNAFU but in our own special British way."

"Good to know," Mulholland said. "Now let's go see if you fixed that Nazi's wagon."

CHAPTER TWELVE

THE SNIPERS EDGED their way past the burning hulk of the German tank, which popped now with exploding rounds like a Fourth of July celebration and smelled disconcertingly like a barbecue, then headed toward the steeple. The road was like the floor of a slaughterhouse with bodies scattered about. The tank tracks had squashed some of the remains into jelly, oozing now into the thick French mud.

The farm boy, Meacham, stopped, put his hands on his knees, and began to vomit.

"That poor chap has got it right," the Brit said. "It's bloody awful, is what it is."

The next landmark they passed was the still-burning wreckage of the Sherman tank. From there, they moved cautiously, just in case the German sniper was still in residence. But the tower had been quiet since the Brit had fired the bazooka at it.

"I think you cooked that Kraut," Vaccaro said.

"We'll see."

They moved on toward the church, spreading out and running one by one from shrubs or whatever cover presented itself. Still, there was no sign of life in the steeple. The bazooka blast, and before that the glancing shot from the Sherman, had done little visible damage to the church tower aside from stripping off the plaster veneer. The stone walls beneath still appeared sound. Built to last centuries, the steeple was indeed largely unscathed.

They crept cautiously toward the church itself, but there was still no sign of Germans.

"Cole and Vaccaro, go check it out," the lieutenant said.

The two men approached the doorway, but paused just outside. "I wonder if there's anybody still in there," Cole said.

"We'll just have to put the tip in and see how it feels," Vaccaro suggested. "I know it always worked with my girlfriend."

"Well, I ain't your girlfriend, and thank God for that. You want to flip a coin?"

"Nah, I got this one." With that, Vaccaro took a quick peek inside. "Nobody."

Both men entered, soon followed by Mulholland

and Meacham. The lieutenant started toward the stairs that led up into the tower, his .45 out and the sniper rifle slung over his shoulder. "Cole, you come with me. We'll go take a look up top. The rest of you stay here. If there's a German up there still, we don't need him tossing down a grenade and wiping out the whole squad. He could do that even if he's wounded."

Peering up into the gloom of the stairway, Lieutenant Mulholland went up one step, and then another, making his way slowly.

Cole followed, his rifle at his shoulder, ready to fire. Gradually, ready at any moment for a German baton grenade to come bouncing down the steps or for a burst of gunfire from above, they wound their way up the stairs.

The view from the top of the bell tower was amazing. They could see the distant, deep blue of the English channel, and around them was spread the French countryside, the fields dotted with dirt lanes, meandering rivers and small villages. Everywhere they looked, American and Allied troopers were moving along the lanes or across the fields. It was the perfect defensive position—a sniper holed up in the steeple could do a great deal of damage until he was eventually brought down. But that wasn't their purpose and the tower wasn't much use to American troops.

Along with the view, they discovered that there were no Germans up here. Not even dead ones.

There were signs, however, that someone had been there recently. A gold-accented cigarette butt lay on the stone floor. Cole picked up one of several brass shell casings. He counted more than twenty spent shells, nearly each one representing an American GI who was now dead in the lane below. One of those rounds had killed Chief. Like the empty brass they had found in the sniper's nest back at the hedgerow, this one had Cyrillic markings. The shots had been fired by a German with a Russian rifle. One who smoked fancy French cigarettes.

Cole held up the shell for the lieutenant's inspection.

"I'll be damned," Lieutenant Mulholland said, once he had spotted the Russian markings. "It appears our sniper friend was at work up here."

"Ain't no friend of mine," Cole said.

"I wouldn't be so sure about that," Mulholland said. "Look at this."

The lieutenant pointed out where, in the wood railing of the belfry tower, the enemy sniper had used a sharp implement, perhaps the tip of a knife, to scratch something into the wood. It was a rough outline of a Confederate flag. Just like the one on Cole's helmet.

"What the hell is that, Lieutenant? Some kind of message?"

"Hell, Cole, I don't know what it means. Maybe he just wants to let you know he let you get away."

Cole knew he must have been in the enemy sniper's sights down on the road, and yet the man had spared him, shooting Chief instead. The German had his scope on Cole long enough to be able to study the Confederate flag on his helmet.

The thought made Cole's flesh crawl. It was as if the German was saving him for later. Cole had done that himself once, hunting in the mountains. There was an old buck deer he had tracked for hours, and when he finally got him in his sights, Cole didn't shoot. He admired the spread of the buck's antlers, supported by a thick neck and powerful shoulders. A damn fine buck.

It wasn't out of pity or remorse for the deer—Cole had no qualms about killing—but he knew that if he killed the buck, he wouldn't be able to hunt it again. It was the kind of self indulgent decision a rich man might make—and it meant Cole had to settle for a couple of squirrels to fill the stew pot.

He'd never come across the buck again, and for all he knew, it was still out there, roaming the mountains back home. Sometimes, laying awake at night in his narrow Army bunk, with the sounds of snoring and farting men around him, Cole had thought about that old buck. He liked to imagine being alone in the cold mountain woods. It was a kind of waking dream you could have, going over that hunt again in your mind. Hunting him again was something Cole looked forward to. In some ways, he reckoned that buck had kept him from going crazy.

Cole hadn't thought of war as hunting. It was different in his eyes. It was about staying alive as much as it was about killing. But what if this German sniper had made it through Russia—the worst kind of fighting, from everything Cole had heard—and now saw war the way Cole had seen that hunting trip? As a game? As a challenge? As a test of one's skills?

A sniper like that had to be very good, very sure of himself. And very deadly. And now the wily son-of-a-bitch was hunting him.

* * *

COLE WAS BORN in 1920 near a place called Gashey's Knob. To call the Cole homestead a house would be a stretch of the imagination. It was a shack with tarpaper siding and rusty metal sheets for a roof. An old wood stove kept it more or less warm—mostly less, to tell the truth—in the winter. There was a front porch where dogs and pigs slept underneath, out of the rain. Sometimes Cole slept there to keep out of the way when his old man was on a bender. Normally, Cole crowded inside the cabin with four skinny younger brothers and sisters, and he went to bed hungry too many times to count.

His father made a kind of living as a trapper and bootlegger, but it wasn't enough to keep the family fed, much less to buy twentieth century conveniences like electricity and indoor plumbing. If you needed to take a shit, you did it in the outhouse out back and wiped your ass with a page torn out of an old Sears Roebuck catalog.

Cole's old man was mean as a rattlesnake and drunk half the time on his own moonshine, and it wasn't until he got to the Army that he realized it wasn't normal for your daddy to beat the hell out of you on a regular basis. For all his faults, Cole's pa was also a skilled outdoorsman, what people would have called a mountain man in an earlier time. When he was sober, he taught Cole what he knew.

In the summer of 1933, times were hard all over the country, but they were pretty much always hard in Gashey's Knob. Cole was somewhere between a boy and a man, like he had one foot on each side of a stream and was wondering which way to step. He would always remember it as the Summer of the Bear, and it was one of his most painful memories.

An old black bear had come down out of the mountains and was lurking around cabins, raiding vegetable patches and breaking into chicken coops.

Likely the bear was old or sick, and driven by hunger. Old man Thompkins had caught a glimpse of the bear sniffing around his hen house. He reckoned that bear weighed 400 pounds, its muzzle scarred and grizzled with gray. He peppered it with bird shot so that now the bear was old, sick, hungry—and mad with pain.

Cole and his pa came across that bear on their way back from squirrel hunting. They were crossing the high meadow to the west of their cabin and there was the bear in the middle of it, blocking their path home, rising out of the tall grass. He had killed a calf and was feeding on the carcass, muzzle dripping gore like something out of a nightmare. The bear stood close to seven feet tall.

He roared and charged.

Cole ran, but you can't outrun a bear. Even an old one can sprint fast as a horse. He could still feel his fear, the taste of it in his mouth like pennies.

He worked his jaw. Spat.

Pa had an old double-barreled shotgun with two double-ought buckshot shells. That was all the ammunition he had. He stood his ground and fired when the bear almost had his nose in the barrel.

Sheepishly, heart pounding, Cole came back to where his single-shot .22 rifle lay in the grass.

"Pick it up," Pa said. "Now give it here. You ain't man enough yet to carry that."

Those words hurt worse than any fist the old man had ever hit him with.

Less than a year later Pa was found shot dead in the mountains. The local sheriff called it a hunting accident, but Cole knew different. Like as not, Pa had been sniffing around someone's still.

Cole became the family provider. They ate what he could shoot or trap, and they ate all right for a change because he turned out to be a good hunter and an even better shot than his old man. Bullets cost hard cash they didn't have, and sometimes he had one bullet, one shot, and those skinny brothers and sisters went hungry if he missed.

Cole did not miss.

Later on he got wind of who killed Pa. Pa had been no good, but blood was blood, and revenge ran through his veins like snow melt down an icy creek.

If it was possible, his father's killer was a meaner rattlesnake than Pa had been. He went gunning for Pa's killer and the two stalked each other for several days in the deep mountain country. Cole walked back out; the other man's body was buried where no one would ever find it.

Back in the mountains, you had time to think. Cole reckoned that he was always trying not to run from that bear. Since then, he had never run from anything. He was already hard and stubborn like a knot of tree root, and the Army training made him even harder. Like his old man, he had dark moods when meanness radiated off him like it did off a stray alley cat.

One day in boot camp he'd had enough of Jackson bullying the other mountain kid, Jimmy Turner, who was as different from Cole as a deer is from a wildcat. He put a can of beans in a sock and caught Jackson alone one night after lights out. Sent him to the infirmary for a few days.

The drill sergeant was no fool and suspected that Cole had done it. "Goddamnit Cole, Jackson is an asshole and he had it coming." He stuck his finger in Cole's face. "But the next soldier you fuck up had better be a German."

Cole had taken the sergeant's message to heart.

CHAPTER THIRTEEN

THE GERMAN SNIPERS slept that night in an old chateau commandeered by the Wehrmacht. The French owners had fled, leaving the German army to inhabit its rooms and grounds. The house was neglected and damp, but it was far better than the cold woods and fields. The mansion had been converted into an indoor campground by hordes of weary, muddy troops. The Germans had also occupied the kitchen, so there was plenty of hot soup and even fresh-baked bread.

As an officer, Von Stenger was able to secure a room that was grand enough to have been the domain of some long-ago Norman baron. The room was able to accommodate Von Stenger, as well as Wulf and Fritz. He took a chance that the chimney still worked and started a small fire in the fireplace, then worked to clean the Russian rifle.

"Do you need help, *Herr Hauptmann?*" Fritz asked.

"A man always cleans his own weapons. Of course, they need to be fired first," Von Stenger said, giving the youthful soldier a sideways look. At the church steeple today, the boy hadn't fired so much as a single shot. He tossed his boots at the boy. "These could do with a shine. Make sure you do it out in the hallway."

Fritz frowned down at the muddy boots. "Yes, sir."

The boy took the boots and went out. Over in his corner, Wulf gave a low laugh. He was cleaning his own weapon, the standard-issue Mauser that had been converted to sniper use with the addition of a telescopic sight.

"Honestly, sir, I don't know where you got him. That boy has his head in the clouds the whole time."

"You might say I inherited him," Von Stenger said, thinking back to his old companion, Willi, whose body was now likely mouldering in some mass grave the Allies had dug. That was duty for you.

"You should send him away, sir," Wulf said. "He will only cause trouble for us."

"He will prove useful when the times comes," Von Stenger said. "Until then, who else would I get to shine my boots?"

Wulf made a guttural, mirthless sound that Von

Stenger took to be a laugh. "Are we going back to the church steeple in the morning, sir?"

"A sniper never returns to the same place if he can help it," Von Stenger said. He was a little surprised Wulf had thought that's what they would be doing, but he reminded himself that while Wulf had been to sniper training, this was his first time in actual combat.

Earlier that day, he had worried briefly about being trapped in the church steeple by the enemy, or perhaps once the American tank opened fire. The tank crew had proved to be terrible shots, and then the Tiger tank had come along and destroyed the Sherman with a spectacular show of German superiority. If that was the best that American tanks could do against Panzers, an awful lot of them were going to be turned into burning wreckage.

He found himself lapsing into the instructor tone he would have taken at the sniper school. "Never use the same sniper's nest two days in a row. Never come and go by the same route. If you can, fire and move on. Those are the rules a sniper must follow if he wishes to survive long on the battlefield."

"Like you, *Herr Hauptmann*?"

"Yes, Wulf, like me."

Fritz appeared in the doorway again. "How many men have you killed, *Herr Hauptmann*?"

Both the boy and Corporal Wulf waited keenly

for his answer, but Von Stenger took so long to respond that they thought it was possible he had not heard the question. Finally, he spoke. "When I began my career, in Spain where we supported General Franco's troops, I used to keep count. It was a matter of pride. And the Spanish were very tough to kill, so that was something."

"How many?"

"Eighty in Spain. Then came Poland. I ran out of bullets because there were so many to shoot."

"You were in Russia," Wulf said. Every German soldier knew that to have fought and survived as a sniper on the Eastern Front was the ultimate test. "That's where you earned your Knight's Cross."

Von Stenger touched the medal, then shrugged. "Well, I gave up counting back in Poland. One begins to realize that a sniper does not kill so many as a few well-placed bombs, but do you think our Luftwaffe bombers worry about their tally? So I stopped counting. There are many ways to determine one's success in war. For example, having done my duty for the Fatherland, I came home from Russia with my life, and with this rifle."

"A Russian sniper rifle."

"Yes," Von Stenger said.

When Von Stenger did not elaborate, the boy said, "I must finish your boots, sir."

"Good, and after you have shined my boots I

want you to find the following four items and bring them to me. A burlap sack, forty feet of rope, a uniform tunic and a helmet."

The boy suddenly looked near panic. "Where am I going to get a uniform and a helmet, sir?"

"From someone who isn't wearing them," he said. "Be resourceful."

Once the boy had left to complete his assignment, Wulf asked, "Sir? What's all that business about with the tunic and helmet?"

"We are going hunting tomorrow for our own kind, and we must have a trap for them."

While the old house was short on warmth, there appeared to be no shortage of wine from the cellars. The boy returned with a bottle as well as the items Von Stenger had requested. They shared the wine by the fire, and then both Wulf and Fritz went to their blankets. The boy curled up and went to sleep instantly, reminding Von Stenger of a dog, legs kicking, mouth hanging open. Only the young could sleep so deeply and artlessly. Wulf was soon snoring in his corner.

Von Stenger hardly thought of himself as old, but in some ways he already had a lifetime of memories, and not all of them were pleasant. Wulf and the boy had asked how many he had killed in his career as a sniper. While he had shot a great number of men— and even women—he could easily recall many of the individual deaths. These memories clung to him and weighed down his mind, fending off sleep like armor.

Restless, he poured more wine, sitting by the fire and smoking, making plans for the morning. It was better to think ahead than dwell on the past. There was no doubt the Americans would attack, and when they did, there would be a trap waiting for them at one of the river crossings.

* * *

"LET'S MOVE OUT," Lieutenant Mulholland said with as much enthusiasm as he could muster, but his voice sounded croaky and tired nonetheless.

The Americans woke up cold and groggy, with any hopes for a hot cup of coffee dashed by the chatter of machine gun fire nearby. The German defenders were hard at work in the early morning light, if they had even slept.

A colonel was making the rounds, handing out orders, the stub of an unlit, well-chewed cigar hanging from his mouth. Mulholland had reported to him last night, making him aware of the sniper squad's presence. "Lieutenant Mulholland, I need you and your men on a counter sniper operation."

"Yes, sir."

"We have us a situation at the La Fiere Bridge," the colonel said. He produced a map, which was damp and badly wrinkled. Taking the cigar out of his mouth, he used it to jab at the map, leaving wet, ashen smudges. "Our boys are trying to get across the Merderet River there, only the Jerries won't let them. We keep throwing more men at it, and they keep throwing more men at it, and meanwhile it's a big goddamn Mexican standoff."

"I understand, sir."

"Do you? Then hell, you are way ahead of me. That bridge should have been taken by oh six hundred on D-Day, and here we are on D plus three still messing around with the Jerries. But you're not going to the goddamn La Fiere Bridge." The colonel stabbed at the map again. "This is a tributary of the Merderet and it's got a much smaller bridge. It's near a village called Caponnet. The bridge is too small for armor because the damn thing would probably collapse under the weight, but we can move some men across and maybe come in behind the Jerries at La Fiere."

"Yes, sir."

"It's the same story there, though, in that the Jerries don't want us to cross the goddamn bridge. I've got reports coming in this morning that the Jerries have it covered with snipers, thick as ticks as a hound dog that's been coon huntin' all night. I need you and your boys to dig 'em out."

Mulholland tried not to reflect on the fact that

his experience as a sniper spanned roughly three days. "We'll sweep it clean, sir."

"You've got a can-do attitude, son, and I like that. Just keep your head down and give those Jerry snipers hell."

Lieutenant Mulholland started to salute, then stopped himself, remembering that it was bad policy. At any rate, the colonel had already moved on. Dawn was breaking, daylight was sweeping over the wood and fields of Normandy's bocage country, and there was much to be done. It looked as if the sun was actually going to show itself today, which would be something, after a string of gloomy, overcast days. Instead of the sound of birdsong, he could hear the distant chatter of small arms fire, growing louder.

Mulholland thought that it was a hell of a thing to watch the sun come up and yet know that you had a good chance of being killed before it set. He tried not to think about that too much.

He looked around for the French girl. She was standing beside Private Cole, sharing a cigarette with him. They both looked up as he approached. For the first time, he noticed that she had flat, black eyes like wet stones. There was certainly nothing soft or feminine in her glance. Cole's eyes couldn't have been more different—clear as a mountain stream on a cold morning. They were just as empty of emotion. It was hard to tell what Cole was thinking, but there was a kind of primal intelligence and cunning in those eyes that unsettled the lieutenant. It was like looking a wolf in the eye.

"*Mademoiselle?* I need you to take us to the Caponnet bridge."

"*Oui.*" She exhaled smoke. "I know the way."

A couple of the men moved off into the brush to relieve themselves, and then they started down the road toward the bridge.

Chief was dead, killed by the sniper in the church steeple. That left the lieutenant, Cole, Jolie, Meacham and the wisecracking Vaccaro. The British airborne trooper had asked to tag along.

"I'll be damned if I'll ever find my bloody unit," he said. "I've yet to see another Brit. It's Americans everywhere I look. Maybe I could join up with your squad, sir."

"Suit yourself, Neville. But we're supposed to be snipers. Are you any good with a rifle?"

Neville hefted his submachine gun. "You worry about the long shots, sir, and I'll take care of the close work. I'm also prepared to grenade Jerries, knife them, garrote them, beat them at poker or drink them under the table as the need arises."

Mulholland had to smile. "All right, Neville. We can use a man of your talents."

"I'm sticking close to this one," Neville said, nodding at Cole. "He looks mean."

Vaccaro spoke up: "What about me? I'm goddamn deadly with this rifle."

"That's what I'm afraid of," Neville said. "Do me a favor, mate, and walk in front of me. I'm a little worried that you might accidentally shoot someone."

"You limeys ought to be glad we're here. Otherwise you'd all be speaking German this time next year."

"Bollocks to that." Neville patted his submachine gun. "We were doing just fine on our own."

Vaccaro snorted. "You live on an island. It's not even like a real country."

"Keep it up, Yank, and I'll save the Jerries the trouble."

"What's that supposed to mean?"

"Knock it off, you two," Mulholland said. "Neville, I didn't make you part of this squad to pick fights with my men."

"Sorry, sir," Neville grumbled.

They moved out. Jolie kept them off the main roads that brought the greatest chance of running into German troops or tanks, leading them down sunken roads between the hedges or dirt lanes that were little more than paths through the countryside. It was clear she knew the territory well, because she never paused to consult a map or compass. The only map she appeared to need was the one in her head.

They soon heard the sound of running water and

came out into a field bordering the tributary of the Merderet River. This smaller river was swollen with spring rains and running swiftly, threatening to overflow its banks and flood the low fields beyond. Though not particularly wide, the river was too swift and deep to wade across. No wonder the bridges were proving so essential, and why the Germans were either blowing them up or fighting tooth and nail to keep them in the hands of their own troops.

They came to another road that curved away from the river, and Jolie led them down it. Before long, they encountered a unit of American airborne troops, hunkered at the base of a towering hedge at a bend in the road. Mulholland found the captain in charge, who looked weary, his face covered in stubble, and asked him what was happening.

"German snipers have us pinned down," he said. He jerked his chin at two bodies that lay fifty feet further along. Another man was in the middle of the narrow bridge, crying out for a medic. "My men went to help him, and it turns out the snipers were using him for bait. We're in their blind spot right now, but when we move toward that bridge we're right in their line of fire. Those poor bastards never had a chance, never knew what hit them. We could rush the bridge, but they would get a hell of a lot of us by the time we got across."

"How many snipers?" Mulholland asked.

"There's one up ahead, and another one in the woods on that hill to the right. I hate these goddamn snipers. Nothing but sneaky bastards." For the first time, the airborne captain seemed to notice the scoped rifle Mulholland was carrying. "Present company excepted. You're on our side, after all. We've captured two Jerry snipers so far, and let's just say they died of lead poisoning before they made it back to the POW processing point."

"We'll have a go at them," Mulholland said.

"Be my guest," the captain said. He shook a cigarette out of a red and white pack, then raised his voice to address his men. "Smoke 'em if you got 'em, boys. We're gonna let someone else have all the fun for a change."

CHAPTER FOURTEEN

WHILE LIEUTENANT MULHOLLAND was talking with the squad leader, Cole took a good look at the countryside. The woods and fields of the bocage were green with spring, and yet the morning gloom managed to make the landscape appear dismal and foreboding. The road meandered toward the bridge, reminding him of one of the winding roads back home, which folks liked to say followed whichever way the cows had wandered back in the old days when livestock and deer made most of the trails.

On the far side of the river was an abandoned mill with a rotting, moss-covered mill wheel that still turned in the current. Beyond the river and mill was an open field that sloped up toward the woods that hid the snipers. Behind the Americans, and before the curve in the road that hid them from the snipers, was a similar hill.

He turned to Jolie. "Is there another bridge across that river?"

"Non," Jolie said. "Not for miles. This is the only way across."

"I was afraid you might say that."

"Bien sur it is the only bridge, which is why the Germans are guarding it."

They were in the bottom of a kind of bowl, with the river running through like a crack. If someone could get up on the high ground, into a tree, they might have a good shot at the enemy snipers. But it was at least 600 feet from the German position— someone would have to be a damn good shot, assuming he even had a target. It was likely that the Germans would be camouflaged and hard to spot.

There were now six in the sniper team, including the Brit and Jolie. It was hard to know how many German snipers they were going up against, but from the sounds of it there were at least two, and the Jerries had the upper hand. They needed a plan. The wounded soldier on the bridge was sobbing in pain.

The sound brought Cole's blood to a slow boil. The wounded man had been left out there as bait. These Jerry snipers were real sons of bitches.

Lieutenant Mulholland came back to them,

looking worried. "These men need to cross this bridge to reach their objective. If we don't neutralize these snipers for them, a lot of them are going to die."

"We can't shoot the Jerries if we can't see 'em, sir," Vaccaro pointed out.

"I know that," Mulholland snapped.

"Sir, I have an idea," Cole said. "Put Meacham and Vaccaro up in those woods behind us. It's good high ground to shoot from and the trees will provide cover. That will give the Jerries something to think about."

"Yeah, and what are you going to do, Cole?" Vaccaro wanted to know. "I'll bet while Meacham and I are getting our asses shot at, you'll be down here playing Tiddlywinks with our French Girl Scout."

"You got nothin' to worry about, Vaccaro," Cole said. "That woods is so far away the Germans won't be able to hit anything—if you're lucky, that is. Of course, you won't be able to hit a damn thing either, but they won't know that."

"Like I said, easy for you to say and me to do."

"Well, once you're up in the trees givin' them Nazis something to think about, what I'm goin' to do is swim that river and get into that old mill on the other side. It's good cover and when you draw the Jerries' fire I'll see where they're hiding at."

"Swim that river?" They all looked at the roiling current. The water ran fast here and looked deep.

Vaccaro sounded incredulous. "You're crazy, Hillbilly."

"All right," Mulholland said. "Cole has a good plan. Let's do it."

Meacham and Vaccaro shed their gear, taking only their rifles, and moved off into the fields, following the hedges to keep out of sight of the German snipers until they worked their way into the trees. Vaccaro was still grumbling as he moved off.

"You're really going to swim that river, mate?" Neville asked.

"I reckon."

"Then you are bloody crazy." Neville smiled. "I like that in a man."

Cole worked his way across the field toward the water, keeping out of sight of the enemy snipers. Jolie came along with him. She was adept at moving silently through the fields, like a cat after a mouse. They moved upstream, to a point where Cole judged he would land near the mill once he factored in the current. The river wasn't very wide—you could pitch a stone across. But the current was racing.

The truth was, Cole mistrusted water. He had been around cold, swift creeks a lot as a boy, trapping muskrats and even beaver, and he knew how dangerous water could be. More than one trapper had been drowned by the weight of his winter clothes and the shock of the cold water when he lost his footing and went under. It was Cole's worst nightmare.

For Cole, the beach landing had been terrifying. He had feared the Nazi machine guns much less than the thought of being pulled under the surf and not coming back up, gasping for breath. As it turned out, it had been a near thing. He stared doubtfully at the swift brown water, and then began to take off his boots.

"I hope you ain't shy," he said to Jolie. He handed Jolie his rifle. "Hold this, will you?"

Boots and socks off, he stripped off his jacket and trousers. All he had on were the khaki military-issue boxer shorts. Thinking about the tug of the current in the river, he might have stripped off the underwear if Jolie hadn't been there. He strapped his utility belt with the ammunition and a sheath knife around his waist.

They had found a board to float the rifle across on. Cole would pull it over with a string. He wished he had plastic or something to wrap the rifle in, like they had done with their M1s during that beach landing, but that couldn't be helped. He shivered; he tried to tell himself it was just from the morning cold.

"I will take your clothes back to the road," Jolie said. She looked him over, noticing how lean and pale he was, but well-muscled with tough, corded muscles across his shoulders and a flat belly. "Good luck."

They waited under cover without saying anything more. Cole started to shiver more intensely, and after a while Jolie spread his jacket across his shoulders to keep off the chill while he waited. Where the hell were Meacham and Vaccaro? They ought to be in position by now. He needed them to start shooting in order to distract the Germans.

Finally, some shots came from the hill at Cole's back. He doubted that Meacham or Vaccaro had much of a target, but what mattered was that they had the attention of the German snipers. One shot, then another, came from the woods that hid the Germans. Two snipers, then.

Cole slipped out from behind cover and slid down the river bank. He had pictured himself easing into the river without so much as a splash, but the bank was so steep that at the last minute he slipped on the mud and went under.

The shock of the cold water forced the air out of his lungs, but he stayed under, fighting the urge to come up for breath. This close to the German snipers, if they had spotted him, he was a dead man if his head popped above the surface of the river.

He struck out for the middle of the river, trailing the string behind him. His eyes were open but he couldn't see a thing in the brown, churning water. Finally, his lungs burning and feeling himself close to panic, he came up for air, bobbing gratefully above the river's surface. He grabbed a lungful of air and forced himself to go under again and swim for the far shore.

The weight of his utility belt combined with the current kept threatening to tug him down, but he kicked upwards. It was too murky to see much but at least he knew that the bubbles would lead him to the surface. He broke through again, gulped more air, and ducked under. *Swim*, he told himself. *Just fix your mind on it and swim.*

His hands struck mud, and he realized he had reached the opposite bank. He let himself come up for air, still praying the enemy snipers would not see him. He was just above the abandoned mill, so that was something. The muddy bank was slick and Cole couldn't seem to get a grip. To his horror, he realized he was being carried directly toward the old water-wheel, which spun fast and furious in the current.

He kicked for all he was worth and flayed his arms, struggling against the pull of the water, but it was like a leaf trying to fly against a hurricane. The force of the water was overwhelming. In another instant, the heavy wooden buckets of the waterwheel would come down on his head.

He reached out, desperately, as the stone foundation of the mill flashed by and caught a length of chain fastened to the stone, perhaps for an old mooring. The rush of the river nearly ripped his arm from its socket, but he didn't let go. He managed to slide the rifle onto the stone landing. Struggling, he got the fingertips of his other hand, and then his fingers, around the chain.

He was able to raise himself out of the water a little at a time, and then he got his toes wedged into the slimy sides of the stone foundation. He dug in his knees next, cutting and scraping them against the stone, until he got enough leverage against the water to pull himself up.

With a final effort, he dragged himself onto the stone landing where boats would have once tied up to load and unload sacks of grain. Bleeding and gasping, shivering uncontrollably and his bare flesh covered in goosebumps, Cole just lay there for a minute, gasping like a fish, glad he was on the far side of the mill, out of sight of the Germans. He glanced toward the far bank, looking for some sign of Jolie, but she had melted back into the fields. The little raft was there, though, and he pulled it across with the string.

Gathering his strength, he lifted himself off the flat stone pier and crept into the dark interior of the abandoned mill, keeping the rifle at the ready. The interior smelled of mice and dust. Someone had stripped most of the machinery, but the largest of the cogs and turnstiles remained. The wood was dark and worn with age, resembling iron more than the oak from which it was made. The stone walls were reassuringly thick, though patches of sky showed through holes in the thatched roof.

He found a window overlooking the field and the woods beyond where the German snipers were hidden. The window had no glass or frame—it was just a slit in the stone wall to let in fresh air and light. He reckoned it was a couple of hundred feet across the field, where the grass had been grazed. Looking around, he spotted three or four dairy cows, clearly dead, bloated and stiff where they lay on their sides. He had seen dead livestock all over Normandy, a result of stray bombs and bullets.

Studying the trees, Cole thought that what they could really use was for a P-51 Mustang to come along and pound the hell out of the Germans in the woods. That didn't seem likely, and so it came down to him and his rifle.

His rifle. He glanced down at the Springfield, which had come through without getting dunked in the river, if not exactly high and dry. He slid open the bolt, removed the clip, and tilted the barrel to drain out any water. Later on, the mechanism would get rusty as hell if he didn't get some oil on it, but that couldn't be helped. What mattered was that he could fire a few shots now and take out the German snipers.

He put his eye to the scope. By some small miracle, no water had gotten into the optics.

The natural thing to do would be to poke his rifle through the window slit. But that would be too obvious if anyone looked at the mill. The Germans might not be expecting anyone in the mill—the bridge was covered and the swift current did not make the river inviting to swim—so their attention would be elsewhere. That would change as soon as Cole took his first shot at them.

Through the thick stone walls, he could still hear firing in the distance. That must be Meacham and Vaccaro giving the Germans something to think about.

Still shivering, Cole found a wooden barrel and turned it upright several feet from the window, then put a stack of old burlap grain sacks on top of the barrel. He considered for a moment, then took out his knife and cut three holes in one of the sacks—one for his head and two for his arms—and slipped it on over his head. He used a length of string to belt the sack around his waist. Not exactly a regulation uniform. The fabric was itchy and dusty, and he probably looked silly as a preacher at a sack race, but his shaking soon stopped.

He used a box as a makeshift seat, and then rested the rifle on top of the barrel, cushioned by the grain sacks. His view of the woods was far more limited, but in the gloom inside the mill he would be invisible to the snipers beyond. They could fire through the slit, of course, but they would be shooting blind.

Cole worked the bolt and fed a round into the chamber, then began to scan the woods for the flash of a German rifle that would give him a target.

CHAPTER FIFTEEN

IN RUSSIA, they had called him *The Ghost*. He came and went unseen—or so it seemed to the enemy. What appeared otherworldly to the Russians had, in fact, been simple preparation. Von Stenger and Wulf were in position long before dawn, having hiked the short distance toward the bridge near Caponnet over a tributary of the Merderet River.

Von Stenger knew it was a likely crossing point for American forces frustrated by the stalemate at the La Fiere bridge. When they tried to cross, he and Wulf would be waiting to pick them off. The two snipers would be able to hold off a fair-sized Allied force, freeing up German forces desperately needed elsewhere.

He'd also brought Fritz along. The boy was useless as a soldier, but he made a good pack horse, carrying food, the spare uniform and helmet and rope, and extra ammunition. Once Von Stenger had hidden himself in the trees, he planned to shoot as many Allied troops as possible without having to worry about resupplying.

"Here is what I want you to do with the uniform," Von Stenger said to the boy, and showed him how to stuff it with pine straw until it had some semblance of a human form. "Now, you climb. You can be a monkey, can't you?"

It was hard to see in the pre-dawn darkness, but Fritz managed to get maybe five meters into the tree, and then lowered a rope. Von Stenger tied the dummy to that and had the boy haul it up. Following the sniper's directions, Fritz perched the dummy on a long branch, then lashed a rifle along the branch, as if the dummy was aiming the weapon.

"Be careful, boy, that rifle is loaded."

Up close, the dummy was not very convincing. But seen from the other side of the river, obscured by trees, the dummy would be enough to fool an American marksman.

A string ran from the trigger of the rifle, then around a branch that served as a fulcrum, and from there down to the forest floor. Von Stenger waited until Fritz had climbed down. "When I tell you to, you pull that string. It will make the rifle fire."

Even in the dim light, Von Stenger could see the

boy's quizzical look. "But Herr Von Stenger, the dummy can't hit anything."

"I don't want the dummy to shoot anything. That's my job and Wulf's. The dummy's job is to get shot. Now pay attention, and pull that string when I tell you to, and not a moment before. You are our eyes on the ground, so shout a warning if someone comes."

"Yes, *Herr Hauptmann.*"

He turned to Corporal Wulf. "You and I will take alternating shots," he said. "You take the first one. They will send a scout across the bridge first—shoot to wound. The legs are good; the belly is better. The others will come out to rescue him, and then we can pick them off."

"What if they all come across the bridge at once, *Herr Hauptmann?*"

"Surely they can't be that stupid," he said. "But if they are, stay with the alternating shots. You never know when someone has the sense to shoot back, and it's best to keep them confused about the target."

Leaving the boy stationed at the foot of the oak holding the dummy—Von Stenger did not bother giving him a weapon, for fear that he might start shooting at shadows and give away the snipers' position prematurely—he and Wulf made their way up into trees approximately fifty meters apart and ten meters or so from the edge of the field. They had a sight line on one another, and could signal the other man if necessary. Little communication would be necessary—they had already worked out that they would make alternating shots to confuse the enemy and keep the Americans from zeroing in easily on their positions. If the Americans did have a competent marksman, the dummy would help confuse him.

The tree with the dummy was just a few meters from Von Stenger, but he was more carefully hidden. He wore a camouflaged smock with a hood to which were secured twigs and branches. Even his rifle was wrapped with brownish canvas strips, into which he had stuck a few springs of leaves. He was straddling a thick limb, wedging himself into the crotch formed by the tree limb and the trunk, and while it was not comfortable, it made a solid shooting platform.

When he was finished, the only part of him visible were his eyes, which were light blue and clear. As the light grew in the east and the darkened landscape revealed itself, those sharp eyes kept a close watch on the bridge two hundred meters distant.

The morning was cold and damp, and being forced to lie still along the tree branch allowed the chill to creep through his bones. Of course, it was nothing like the cold of Stalingrad. Religious people liked to say that hell was full of fire and brimstone, but they were wrong. Hell was a cold place, full of ice and snow and Russian snipers who could shoot the eye out of a running hare at 100 meters. Von Stenger preferred Normandy.

The snipers did not have long to wait. The birds had started in the trees, singing in oblivion of the war going on around them, and the light grew stronger. A lone soldier appeared on the narrow bridge, moving slowly forward. He looked somewhat ridiculous, hunched under a heavy pack and with branches stuck into the netting that covered his salad bowl of a helmet, but Von Stenger knew better—the soldier was probably American airborne, a very tough unit.

They let the scout advance halfway across the bridge. Von Stenger had his crosshairs on him, just in case, but then Wulf's rifle fired off to his left. The soldier on the bridge went down as if someone had kicked his legs out from under him. He started to crawl back across the bridge, and his panicked cries for help carried across to the woods.

Von Stenger only had to wait a few seconds until two soldiers came running to drag their wounded man to safety. He waited for one soldier to lean over his companion and grab hold of the back of his pack to start dragging him, then settled the crosshairs on the soldier's knee and squeezed the trigger. The soldier went down screaming.

Wulf shot the other soldier through the belly.

No one else came across the bridge. He was thinking that the three wounded men were doing more to discourage anyone from crossing the bridge than the presence of a Panzer tank.

The soldiers lay there, calling out piteously for help. Their cries barely registered in Von Stenger's mind. He had long since hardened his heart to such things.

The morning grew brighter, and in the distance the chatter of small arms fire and the boom of artillery increased. That would likely be the skirmishing at La Fiere, he thought, or one of several vicious battles taking place in unnamed fields all across Normandy.

On their bridge, nothing happened. One of the wounded men managed to drag himself almost off the bridge and onto the road, but Von Stenger put the crosshairs on the man's belly and gut shot him. He had lain like that for hours, alive, but too weak to do anything. It was a little trick he had learned in Russia. Perhaps the Americans would be foolish enough to send someone to try and snatch him to safety.

Von Stenger had brought along a flask of coffee and a ham sandwich. He drank the coffee and ate, keeping an eye on the bridge and road. It was only a matter of time before the Americans tried something. They had to get across that bridge, after all.

After a while the coffee worked its way through and he shifted around so that he could urinate without leaving his sniper's nest. Below, Fritz looked up in surprise at the sound of Von Stenger's stream spattering the forest floor.

He had been waiting for something to happen, and finally it did. Someone started shooting from the hill on the other side of the river, above the road. He had to admit it was a good position, one that offered a commanding view of the bridge and road, and as he and Wulf had done, the American snipers had climbed into the trees. They kept up a steady fire, but for the life of him, Von Stenger couldn't decide what they were shooting at other than the woods itself. Occasionally a bullet came singing in among the trees, ricocheting madly off the trunks, but obviously the American snipers had no target.

Von Stenger decided to give them one.

By then, he had picked out one of the American snipers. He was firing so often that it was fairly easy to locate him. The Americans seemed to be making an attempt to provide covering fire for the troops at the bridge. Through his telescopic sight, Von Stenger could easily see the American. He was not very well hidden because he had set up shop in a tree that had an open avenue through the branches that gave him a clear field of fire—but that also made him visible. He appeared to be a big, bulky fellow.

All indications were that the snipers were not very experienced. However, that did not necessarily mean that they were poor shots. He understood that

Americans were, for the most part, far more familiar with guns than Europeans. They were a people who liked to hunt and shoot. Back in the encounter with the snipers in the field, the one with the Confederate flag on his helmet had come close. Too close. Given a target, these snipers in the trees might prove very capable. The distance from the trees occupied by the Germans to those occupied by the Americans was not unreasonable for a capable marksman. Von Stenger did not plan on giving the snipers more of a target than he had to.

"Fritz," he called down, without taking his eye from the sight. "Are you paying attention?"

"Yes, *Herr Hauptmann.*"

"I want you to start counting out loud to ten. Count slowly and speak so that I can hear the numbers. Exactly when you say ten, I want you to pull that cord and fire the rifle in the tree. Understand?"

"Yes, sir. When do I start counting?"

"Now."

"Yes, sir," the boy said. "One ..."

Von Stenger had not taken his eye off the American in the tree. It was always a strange experience to be watching someone through the rifle scope, because one part of your brain wanted to accept that he could also see you, especially when the other man's rifle was pointed in your direction.

The boy was counting out loud: "Two ..."

The American's rifle flashed and another crack of a rifle shot reached Von Stenger's ears, but he was confident that the man was not shooting at him.

"Three ..."

Through the high-powered optics, he could see the American's strong jawline and heavy features. The best snipers tended to be smaller, compact men —or women as had been the case in Stalingrad. They could hide more readily and had a lower center of gravity. This fellow was much too big for the job.

"Four ..."

Von Stenger calculated the distance as being perhaps 200 meters. There was very little wind. His rifle was sighted in for 100 meters, and so he elevated the crosshairs ever so slightly to a point high on the American's helmet.

"Five ..."

Due to the gravity of the earth, a bullet began falling soon after it was fired from a gun. The greater the distance it had to travel, the greater the drop. To compensate, a sniper had to elevate his rifle barrel to send the bullet in a higher arc.

"Six ..."

To illustrate the science involved to his students at the sniper training school, Von Stenger had some-times used the example of the American sport of baseball. When the catcher wanted to get the ball to the first baseman, he threw a short, quick throw that had a relatively flat trajectory and beat the runner to base. If someone was throwing a ball to the catcher that had been hit into the outfield, the outfielder threw the ball in a higher arc because it had to cover a greater distance. A ball thrown horizontal to the field was pulled down by gravity before it could reach the catcher.

"Seven ..."

A bullet traveled at much higher speed and far greater distances than a baseball, but the same rules applied.

"Eight ..."

The tree made an ideal rest for the rifle, which was padded with canvas camouflaging and resting directly on the limb. Von Stenger imagined how the limb was connected to the tree trunk, which reached down to the roots, deep in the earth. The hardest shots were those made from a standing position, without benefit of any support. This shooting position was nearly ideal. The crosshairs did not waver.

"Nine ..."

Keeping the crosshairs positioned at the crest of the helmet, Von Stenger let out his breath. His finger took up tension on the trigger, so gently that he was barely aware he was doing it.

"Ten ..."

With the last fraction of tension, the firing pin

was released, springing forward to strike the center of the cartridge in the chamber. The primer exploded, igniting the powder, and the resulting explosion launched the bullet, the rifled barrel putting a spin on the slug that kept it on course during its flight, giving it a deadly accuracy.

In the tree nearby, Von Stenger was dimly aware of the dummy rifle firing at the same instant.

Traveling at nearly 2,800 feet per second, Von Stenger's bullet punched through the front of the American sniper's steel helmet, bored through the skull, and buried itself in the soft tissue of the American's brain. The fool hadn't tied himself into the tree, and the complete loss of muscle control at the moment of death caused the body to slide off the limb and fall to the forest floor as heavily as a sack of potatoes.

A bullet zipped nearby, fired from the trees across the river, but the dummy ruse had worked, confusing the other shooter.

Wulf took the opportunity to fire at the remaining American sniper, but the man must have had the sense to hide himself better than his unlucky companion.

Von Stenger was smiling to himself, secretly pleased. That's when the other bullet came in and killed Wulf.

He heard the corporal grunt in pain and then saw

him go limp. Wulf had tied himself into the tree, so he did not fall. His dead hands still gripped the rifle wedged into a fork in the branches.

Scheisse!

Even now, Von Stenger might be in the enemy rifleman's sights. He felt his insides freeze. Checkmate. Game over.

CHAPTER SIXTEEN

VON STENGER HELD HIS BREATH, expecting the fatal shot at any moment. The seconds ticked by, and Von Stenger was surprised still to be alive. The cold dagger in his belly thawed.

The American sniper had not seen him, after all. But the shot that killed Wulf had come from some-place close. Directly in front of their position. From this side of the river.

Where was the American sniper? The field leading down to the river was empty. He used the scope to scan the river bank. There was little brush along the bank because cattle had grazed right to the edge of the river. No good cover there. He would have seen someone crouched along the bank with a rifle. Then his gaze settled upon the dilapidated mill house. Had someone swum the river and gotten in there? Impossible.

But the more he thought about it, the more it made sense. The thick stone walls of the mill would be like a fortress. He had considered it for their own sniper's den, and just as quickly dismissed it, because the view of the countryside was limited. These trees on the hill gave a much more commanding view.

Where would a sniper be? The only position was the slit window facing the field. Von Stenger saw no one there, but one of the Americans could have set up in there a few feet back from the window, where he couldn't be seen. It's what he himself would have done. *Clever, clever.*

He considered his options. His sniper position, so carefully chosen, was now compromised. If he fired again, the sniper in the mill was close enough to spot his muzzle flash. The dummy rifle ruse had been played.

He could possibly send Fritz into the tree to reload the rifle, but it was better not to use the same trick twice.

Besides, a better use for the boy suddenly came to him.

Slowly, slowly, he unwound himself from his position. Any sudden movement might attract the eye of the American sniper in the mill. Von Stenger had chosen well, however, because he was deep enough into the woods that no one in the mill could see his movements as he climbed down.

Once on the ground, he realized he had been holding his breath.

"Fritz, I want you to do two things. The first one is to go and retrieve the rifle that we used with the decoy and bring it to me. The second is to fetch the medical kit." He added, "And keep your head down."

The boy was soon back with the rifle. The Mauser was standard issue with iron sights, but it would serve the purpose that he had in mind. Von Stenger checked to make certain that the barrel was not obstructed and that the action was clear.

He walked over to check on Wulf, who was clearly dead. A little blood trickled down and spattered on the forest floor. Out of professional interest, he observed that Wulf appeared to have been struck in the head. Good shooting. Whoever was down in that mill knew his business.

Now that he had escaped immediate death, Von Stenger felt a frisson of excitement. A challenge was always welcome.

The sniper had known Wulf just three days and thought that the corporal had been competent. Too bad he was dead. *So many dead,* Von Stenger thought. Several faces flashed in his memory, comrades claimed by the war, and he pushed the image aside. Now was not the time to dwell on that.

He was on his own again, but that was all right. He had always worked better on his own.

He turned to the boy, who had returned with the medical kit. "Come here. Take hold of the rifle like this." The sniper showed him how to grip the weapon in a shooting position, butt against the boy's shoulder, finger on the trigger, left hand cradling the forestock. He worked the bolt and put a round in the chamber. "Now, stay still."

Working quickly but methodically, he used the medical tape from the kit to secure the boy's hands to the rifle.

"Sir, what are you doing?"

"I am making you into a soldier! Now be quiet, or I will tape your mouth shut as well."

"Yes, sir."

When Von Stenger was finished, it looked as if the boy held the rifle ready to fire. It would be convincing from a distance. The Mauser was not semi-automatic, so the bolt had to be worked to reload the rifle. The tape prevented Fritz from doing that. This meant the boy would get one shot.

"Here is what I want you to do," Von Stenger said. "You will walk out of the woods and across the field toward the mill. Straight at it, mind you. There is one round in the chamber. When you are very close, so close you cannot miss, you are to fire through that window. In your case, I would say a distance of ten meters would be about right."

"*Herr Hauptmann*, there is an American sniper in that mill. He shot Corporal Wulf. Did you not know that?"

"Exactly. I need you to distract him. Walk straight toward him. Do not run. Give him some time to notice you."

"Notice me?" Fritz's eyes grew wide. "But sir—"

"I will be here in the woods with my rifle, covering you. If you do not do exactly as I have explained, I will shoot you myself. And I never miss."

The boy had gone pale. Von Stenger had wondered if he had as much between the ears as a rabbit, but it was clear he knew that he had just been given orders for a suicide mission. If the American sniper did not shoot him, Von Stenger would.

Von Stenger positioned himself behind a good-sized log on the forest floor, using the log to steady the rifle. "Now go."

The boy stepped out of the woods. Von Stenger trained the crosshairs on the black slit of the mill window, waiting for the American sniper to reveal himself.

WHAT THE HELL?

Cole watched in disbelief as a German sniper walked out of the woods. A slew of possibilities ran through his mind. Cole wondered if the German was challenging him to a duel. Maybe the German planned to surrender? But the Jerries he had seen so far in Normandy weren't the surrendering type. Besides, this one had a firm grip on his rifle, holding it as if he expected to use it as soon as he found a target.

Didn't the Jerry know he was a dead man walking, out in the open like that?

Cole kept his eye pressed tightly against the rifle scope. He didn't know for sure what was going on, but he didn't like it one bit. Not so long ago he had been shivering, but now sweat ran down his sides from his armpits, making the rough material of the grain sacks itch. He didn't dare scratch for fear the movement would give him away.

One thing for damn sure, if there was still a sniper in those woods, his crosshairs were on the mill window.

Cole's sweat ran faster.

* * *

THE AIRBORNE TROOPS taking shelter on the road couldn't really see what was happening in the field, but up in the woods on the American-held side of the river, Vaccaro did have a clear view. He was also mad as hell that Meacham was dead, and feeling vengeful. It wasn't that he had known Meacham all that well, but he was one of their own, goddamnit.

When he saw the German heading down the hill toward the mill, it was like a gift. Vaccaro wasn't the best shot in the world, but with the crosshairs settled on the German he thought it would be hard to miss.

Vaccaro tightened his finger on the trigger.

He fired before the German sniper had taken five steps out of the woods. But Vaccaro hadn't been able to hit three empty liquor bottles from 100 feet back on the beach. His skills fell short of hitting a real live walking German from more than 600 feet. The bullet kicked up dirt five yards from the soldier's feet. The soldier seemed to stumble, and he looked back at the woods, but then he kept coming straight at the mill. Walking, not running.

That Jerry has either got some brass balls or he's the biggest idiot to ever cross the Rhine, Vaccaro thought.

He put his eye to the scope again. This time, he aimed a little higher.

* * *

DOWN IN THE MILL, Cole held his fire.

It made no sense to him that the Jerry kept

coming. Up on the hill, Vaccaro or Meacham fired again. The shot smacked off a tree trunk somewhere behind the Jerry. Had to be Vaccaro. Hell, that city boy really couldn't shoot for shit. What about Meacham? Had one of the German snipers gotten lucky and taken him out?

The next shot from the hill answered his question. It went wide, kicking up dirt and grass.

Definitely the city boy.

The German sniper was halfway across the field, walking faster now that the bullets were zipping in, but not quite running.

Cole put his crosshairs on the German's chest. The soldier's face sprang up close. The face in the optics belonged to a fresh-faced boy, who looked scared as hell.

This wasn't some Nazi fanatic or battle-hardened soldier. There was a lot of baby fat in that face—evidence of yet another boy who had been caught up in war and didn't belong there, only this one was German. Cole couldn't help but think of Jimmy. Another lamb to the slaughter.

Looking closer, that's when Cole saw the tape on the German's hands. Was the boy wounded? Hell no, somebody had taped his hands to the rifle.

Cole couldn't figure that one, but the young sniper was getting within can't miss range of the mill.

Forty feet. Thirty feet. The Jerry pointed the rifle at the mill window.

With the crosshairs still on the German, his finger began to squeeze the trigger. If the Jerry came two steps closer—

The chatter of machine gun fire interrupted his concentration. Off to his right was another slit window and through it he had a view of the bridge. The Brit, Neville, was charging across, submachine gun spraying bullets toward the woods. He stopped at the wounded man, grabbed him by the back of the collar, and started dragging him to safety.

All of a sudden, the bridge filled with men as the Airborne troops swarmed across, peppering the woods with fire. Someone lobbed a rifle grenade into the trees, and it detonated with a wood-splitting crack as a small tree or branch splintered. No return fire came from the woods.

Then soldiers ran past the mill, charging toward the woods. Jolie tagged along at their rear. One of the soldiers swung toward the mill and leveled his weapon at the German. The fact that the boy was pointing his rifle at the ground kept the soldier from shooting him instantly.

"Drop it, Jerry! Goddamnit, I said drop it! *Dropenzie!*"

The German did not drop the rifle, but he was shaking his head wildly and saying, *"Nein! Nein!"*

"Dropenzie!"

Cole came out of the mill and stepped between the soldier and the German. "He can't *dropenzie*. His goddamn hands are taped to the rifle."

"What the hell?"

The soldier went up and grabbed for the rifle, but only managed to pull the boy off his feet. He went down on his knees. Cole took out a knife. The German kid gasped and shut his eyes. Cole cut the rifle free. "I bet the damn thing ain't even loaded."

"Of course it's frickin' loaded!" the paratrooper said. "He's a goddamn German sniper! There's only one way to deal with a sniper. No prisoners."

The soldier aimed his rifle at the boy's head. The young soldier looked up, his voice choked with fear, and said, "No, please!"

"Christ, he speaks English! Sneaky bastard."

"Don't shoot him," Cole said.

"What do you mean, don't shoot him? You saw what he did to our boys on the bridge. Shot them and left them to die!"

"He ain't the sniper that done it."

"How do you know?"

"Look at him," Cole said. "Does he look like much of a stone-cold Nazi killer to you?"

The soldier looked like he might still shoot the boy. Jolie stepped forward and said, "Cole is right.

There are many real soldiers to kill, but this boy is not one of them."

Jolie's presence seemed to cool the soldier off. "Aw, hell, he's your problem now," he said, and ran off to join the men who were searching the woods. Someone yelled something about there being a dead sniper in a tree.

Jolie said something to the boy in German.

"What are you jabbering on about?" Cole demanded. "I didn't know you spoke Kraut."

"It is a useful skill to speak the enemy's language," she said. "I told him to stay down on his knees with his hands on his head, and that if he tried to run you would shoot him."

"Huh. Is that right? You got yourself a rifle. You can shoot him."

"You are the soldier."

"Yeah, but I ain't an executioner."

"You shot those prisoners on the beach."

"My blood was up," Cole said. "Those sons of bitches killed a lot of good men on the beach. This kid didn't have nothin' to do with that."

Jolie spoke to the boy again in German, then turned to Cole. "There."

"What?"

"I told him you want to shoot him, but I talked you out of it. What do you Americans call it? Good cop, bad cop?"

"You're pretty clever for a French girl," Cole said. "But why do I have to be the bad one?"

"That is simple," Jolie said. "You look mean and crazy, especially because you are wearing a grain sack."

"Huh. I don't suppose you brought my clothes along?"

Jolie smiled and handed him a haversack. "Right here."

He shucked off the grain sack and stood there in his wet boxer shorts, tugging his uniform back on. Being in the Army a few months made you the opposite of shy.

"Come on," he said once he was dressed. "I want to have a look at this dead sniper. Tell this kid here to come along and to keep his hands up. If he runs, I really will shoot him."

CHAPTER SEVENTEEN

THEY MOVED across the field and into the woods, joining the soldiers who were already there. In the wake of the attack across the bridge, there was maybe a quart of adrenaline still pumping through their veins, making the soldiers hyper and jumpy.

Most of the men were gathered around a tree, staring up at the dead German sniper. It appeared he had roped himself into the tree to prevent himself from falling if he was merely wounded. The dead German's mouth hung open and his eyes stared wide like some grotesque Cheshire cat.

Now that the tension of the attack was over, some of the airborne troops lowered their weapons and lit cigarettes, studying the corpse in the tree with professional interest.

"I guess Nazi snipers really do grow on trees," one paratrooper said.

"You wouldn't be going out on a limb if you said he was dead," quipped another.

The jokes were bad and tasteless, but it was a way for the men to blow off steam.

"Who wants to climb up there and cut him down?" Lieutenant Mulholland asked.

Cole liked the lieutenant, but he had noticed that the officer had a bad habit of phrasing an order as a question when he wasn't sure of himself. And sometimes he just plain had some bad ideas.

"To hell with that, Lieutenant," Cole said.

"It's the decent thing to do, Cole. We're soldiers, not barbarians."

Cole spat into the pine needles. "You saw how that Jerry gut shot those boys on the bridge and let them suffer. I reckon he can stay up there and rot. They got buzzards here, same as home."

There was a tense silence as Mulholland looked from the tree to the hardened faces around him, and then back at the tree again. After a while he just shook his head and walked away.

Corporal Neville came over and one of the Americans gave him a cigarette. "You are one crazy Tommy," the American said. "The way you rushed that bridge—well, you're damn lucky you're not dead."

"I couldn't stand leaving those wounded men out there another minute." Neville nodded up at the tree. "This lot here were using them for bait to draw us out. Besides, I'm not half as crazy as this hillbilly here. He swam the river and took out the snipers for us."

One of the paratroopers looked at Cole. "That must feel good, huh, knowing you got one."

Cole looked up into the tree and shrugged. He had shot this man, killed him with a single bullet, and he looked inside himself for some feeling about that, but he felt nothing—neither good nor bad about it. It was pretty much the way he felt about killing a fox— it was simply something that needed killing.

The paratrooper had more to say: "If you ask me, we ought to grease that little Nazi right over there. He's a sniper too, which I don't count as a regular prisoner."

Cole flicked his cigarette away so he could get both hands on his rifle. He settled his ice chip eyes on the paratrooper. "I captured him, so I reckon that makes him my prisoner, and I ain't goin' to let you shoot him."

"Easy there, Reb," the paratrooper said, taking a step back from Cole. "I'm just saying, is all. If you want him, then hell, you can have him. He's your prisoner."

Cole looked over at the German kid—who dutifully kept his hands on his head—and noticed that the German kept looking around the woods as if searching for someone.

"Jolie, jabber at that boy and ask him who he's looking for," Cole said to their guide.

Jolie did just that, asking a few questions in German. The boy answered at length and with some excitement, gesturing wildly, and talking to the point that Jolie finally had to cut him off.

"What's he goin' on about?"

"He says there was another sniper, but the boy doesn't see him, so he must have gotten away. Fritz here says that one's name is Captain Von Stenger, and he is some kind of super sniper. His nickname is The Ghost. He taught at the sniper training school and he fought against the Russians on the Eastern Front. The boy says this sniper is the one who shot Chief— and one of our snipers up on the hill."

Cole walked over to where the boy had been pointing. He looked up and had a start when he saw what he thought was someone in a tree overhead. But as he swung his rifle up he saw that it was only a dummy made out of a German uniform stuffed with pine needles. Up close it wasn't very convincing, but seen at a distance through a rifle scope it would have fooled him. Cole's position in the mill had kept him from seeing anything but the two rifle flashes, but the dummy would have tricked Vaccaro and Meacham, who had a clearer view up on the hill. Cole had gotten lucky in shooting the real sniper.

Cole couldn't help but be impressed by how sly these Germans were. The boy had said the other German was some kind of super sniper. He reckoned the boy was right.

He walked among the trees, looking for some clue as to where this sniper had been hidden. Something bright winked at him from the mossy forest floor, and he stooped to pick up a spent brass rifle cartridge. The base was marked with the strange Cyrillic characters.

"I'll be damned," he said. He looked around some more and spotted one of the gold-tipped stubs of a fancy French cigarette, just like the ones he had found in the sniper's nest back at the hedgerow and in the church steeple. It was too much to be a coincidence. They had to be dealing with the same sniper here.

Cole waved Jolie and the boy over. "Tell me more about this Von Stenger," he said. "I have a bad feeling that we're goin' to run into him again."

"There is a good chance of that," Jolie agreed. "According to our prisoner here, Von Stenger is bivouacked in an old chateau. I know just where it is."

"Considering that it's probably surrounded by Jerries and Tiger tanks, that don't do us much good."

Jolie showed her teeth in a smile. "Leave that to me," she said.

"What are you planning to do?"

"Kill him," she said. "What else would I do with him? But first, I want you to give me a shooting lesson."

* * *

Soon after they had overrun the snipers' nest, the paratroopers prepared to move on. Their captain shook hands with Lieutenant Mulholland, then tried to talk Neville into coming with them.

"We're heading for St. Lo to link up with the rest of the 101st Airborne. We could use a crazy Tommy bastard like you," their captain said. "We lost a lot of good men in the drop."

"Thanks, mate, but all the same I think I'll stay on with this lot," he said. "They've done a fair job so far of killing these bloody Germans."

"Cheerio then."

Neville laughed. "You Yanks catch on to the lingo fast. Stick with it and we'll have you speaking proper English in no time."

The American paratroopers drifted away through the trees and out into the open fields, toward the not-so-distant sound of machine gun fire and the *whump, whump* of artillery rounds.

The snipers stayed right where they were because the woods offered good cover until they could decide what to do next.

The lieutenant spotted Vaccaro coming across the bridge and waved him toward the woods. He had made it back from where he had been positioned in the woods on the high ground across the river.

"Meacham?" the lieutenant asked, but Vaccaro only shook his head. For once, he didn't seem to have a wisecrack handy.

"He never had a chance," Vaccaro finally said. "That Jerry sniper picked him off from way over here? Damn, but that German can shoot. I climbed up and got the body down and put him beside the road." He nodded at the German. "Maybe we should get him to go back and dig the grave."

"There will be a burial detail coming by," the lieutenant said, though how he knew that was hard to say. "We'll eat here and take a rest. At least we know it's clear of Germans."

"Well, we got us a Jerry right here from the looks of it," Vaccaro pointed out.

"He's just a dumb kid who's barely old enough to shave," the lieutenant said. "We can keep an eye on him. It's only the rest of the German Army that we have to watch out for."

* * *

IT TURNED out that the German soldier's last name was Fritz. Now that it was becoming clear that the Americans didn't plan to shoot him, his fear had given way to a puppy-like cheerfulness. If he'd been a dog, Mulholland was sure the boy would be happily licking all their faces and wagging his tail. Instead, he kept bouncing around with a happy grin.

He knew a smattering of English, but they relied on Jolie to question him further in German. Based on what she found out, the puppy quality made sense. Their German prisoner was just sixteen years old, one of the young recruits that the increasingly desperate Wehrmacht was bringing in to fill the depleted ranks even as the enemy pressed in from two fronts. It was more than evident that the boy was no member of the Hitler Youth or any sort of fanatic. He was just a kid who found himself far from home in a place he really didn't want to be.

They opened up C rations, sat on stumps or logs, and began to eat. When it was clear that they were taking a break for some chow, the kid set about building a fire and boiling water for coffee—the rations each came with a packet of instant. Cole handed the kid a can of cubed turkey, and he wolfed it down.

Each of them, in their own minds, reminded themselves that this kid was the enemy, though it was hard to take the boy seriously as any kind of threat.

Mainly, he seemed happy to be alive. His cheerfulness was a little infectious.

"That goddamn Meacham," Vaccaro said. "He was all right. If you've got to go, you know, one quick bullet is the way to go out. Pop. He never felt a thing."

Crouched over the fire, waiting for the water to boil, the German kid was now trying out his English. "Hey, Yank!" he said. "Baseball! Apple pie!"

Jolie turned to Cole. "How about that shooting lesson?"

CHAPTER EIGHTEEN

"THE FIRST THING you need is a decent rifle," Cole said.

"What is wrong with this one?"

He studied the ancient hunting rifle in her hands. The stock was scarred and the barrel, though it had been cleaned and oiled, showed signs of once having been pitted with rust. It was a single shot, bolt action rifle with iron sights, and probably none too accurate. The Germans had confiscated all French hunting rifles, so this was the best the Resistance could scrounge up to fight the occupiers. Considering all the weaponry available since the landing, he was a little surprised that no one had provided her with a better rifle.

"C'mon," he said. "I got an idea."

He led her over to the tree that held the dead

German sniper. No one had wanted to climb up and cut him down, which in hindsight was a good thing, from Cole's point of view. It meant that no one had gotten his hands on the dead German's scoped Mauser K98. He shimmied up the tree and in no time had claimed the sniper rifle.

"You are good at climbing trees," Jolie said once he was back on the ground.

"I used to do a little coon huntin'," he said. "Sometimes you have to go up after 'em if you can't get a clear shot."

"Coon? What is coon?" Jolie looked perplexed.

"You know, raccoon. Back home we called them mountain bandits."

"Ha! I like that name. We call them *raton laveur*."

"*Raton?* Like in rat?"

"Yes, *raton*. And *laveur* means wash." Jolie rubbed her hands together in a washing motion. She laughed. "The washing rat!"

Cole shook his head. "I reckon that's French for you. Calling a raccoon a washing rat."

"And where does raccoon come from? Is that an English word?"

"It comes from an Indian word way back."

"Ha! I am going to call you *le raton laveur* if you are not careful. So come, what is your given name? You already know mine."

"Micajah."

Jolie considered that. "Hmm. Well, it is a better name than *raton*."

"Thanks, I reckon."

He gave the dead German's rifle a once over, working the bolt, checking the barrel, and then reinserting the stripper clip of five 7.92×57 mm cartridges. He handed it over to Jolie. "Try that on for size. The Jerries make a decent rifle. It's a whole lot better than grandpa's shootin' iron you got there. You won't never have no shortage of ammunition. All you got to do is pick some off a dead German. Lots of 'em around, in case you ain't noticed."

"It is ironic, using the Germans' own guns to shoot them."

"You know, back home there's a famous explorer folks still talk about named Daniel Boone, and he once said that all a man needs to be happy is a good rifle, a good horse, and a good woman."

"I know you have a good rifle, but what about the horse and the woman?"

"Why?" Cole couldn't help grinning. "You know where I can get me a good horse?"

Jolie snorted again. "I was thinking more about the woman, but maybe we can find you a horse if that is what you prefer. Perhaps a donkey would suit you best. How do you say it? A jackass."

Lieutenant Mulholland saw them talking and wandered over. "What have you got there?" he asked.

"A new rifle," Jolie said. "Your hillbilly sniper here is about to give me a shooting lesson."

"*Mademoiselle*, I would be happy to show you how to shoot."

"Lieutenant, that is very kind. I do not wish to trouble you. Micajah has already said he would teach me."

"Micajah?" The lieutenant blinked in puzzlement. "Who is that?"

"Why, that is your sniper's name. You did not know?"

"I guess I already forgot it. Apparently you two know each other pretty well," the lieutenant said sourly. He struggled to keep from sounding huffy. "I guess Cole—Micajah—is the man for the job."

"He has a very good eye."

"In more ways than one, apparently."

"I am sorry, but I do not understand."

"Oh, never mind. Just make sure you two don't attract unwanted attention from any Jerry patrols."

The lieutenant moved off to where Fritz was poking at the fire, preparing to boil another pot of coffee.

"I think your lieutenant is jealous. *Il est jaloux*."

"Jealous of what?"

"Of you teaching me to shoot. What else? I believe he would like that job for himself."

Cole smirked.

"I hope he does not cause trouble for you."

"No, the lieutenant ain't like that. He's all right."

"What about you? Do you play by the rules?"

"You mean there's rules? I'll be damned. Now come on, let's go teach you to shoot."

They left the shelter of the woods and crossed the field toward the old mill. At the water's edge some farmer had erected a fence years before to keep live-stock out of the river. Most of the crosspieces had rotted away from neglect, but the bleached, weath-ered posts still stood upright. Cole paced off 200 feet from the posts and motioned Jolie over.

"I have only shot a gun a few times," Jolie admit-ted. "We never had much ammunition and we did not want to give ourselves away. The SS was always on the lookout for the Resistance."

"The first thing you want to do is make friends with your rifle," Cole said. He then showed her how to load and unload the Mauser, and then how to work the bolt action.

"You want I should stand up?"

"That's a good start for our lesson," Cole said. "But it's very hard to hit anything from a standing position. The rifle gets heavy. Your aim starts to wobble. The best thing you can do is lay that rifle across anything you can find to steady it so all you have to worry about is your aim. Now, put it to your shoulder, tight, so that you move with the recoil and don't have the rifle butt slamming into your shoulder. Put your eye up near the scope, but not right up against it. Otherwise, when that rifle goes off and kicks back that scope will whack into your eye and you will start to look like one of them *raton leveurs*. Sometimes you can't avoid it, which is why a lot of snipers have bruises around their eyes."

"Is that how you knew Fritz was not a sniper?"

"That, and the fact that his hands were taped to his rifle." Cole smirked. "That's generally a sign of someone who don't want to be holding a rifle in the first place."

"You would not let the other soldiers shoot him. Why not?"

"He reminds me of someone," Cole said, thinking of Jimmy, killed that first morning on Omaha Beach. There was someone else who didn't belong in the war. Nobody had taped his hands to a rifle, but Jimmy had been put on a landing craft with a one-way ticket for Omaha Beach, which amounted to the same thing. "Besides, I suppose there's been enough killin' these last few days, though there's bound to be more."

Jolie nodded. "What is the next step?"

"You find your target. Look through the sight. Do you see that fence over yonder? Aim for one of them posts."

"All right."

"Now, the thing about shooting is that you've got to ease up on your shot. Keep your aim on the post, but you'll see your crosshairs float around. It's hard to hold steady."

"Merde," she muttered. "This is true."

"Keep your finger on the trigger. All you want on there is the pad of your finger. Take a breath. Let it out. Take another breath and hold it in. Let it out and take another one if you got to. Let the crosshairs do their little dance. All the time, your finger is taking up some more tension on the trigger. You get used to a rifle after a while and you know when it's almost goin' to fire. When your crosshairs drift onto that post, let your finger take up that last bit of tension, gentle like you were pulling on a baby's hair."

Jolie breathed, let it out, breathed again. When the rifle fired, it actually surprised her.

"I missed!"

"Well, that fence post ain't crossed the field yet to bayonet us. I reckon you've got time for another shot."

Jolie worked the bolt, ejecting the empty shell and feeding a live round into the breech. She pressed the rifle tight to her shoulder. She felt Cole leaning in close, pressing against her. She could feel his breath on her cheek and his voice murmuring in her ear. "All right, I just want to see what you see through the scope. Those crosshairs do dance, don't they? Let me help."

His rough hands slipped over her own, steadying the rifle. There was something intoxicating about having him pressing close against her. None of them had washed much these last few days, living rough, and she could smell him—it wasn't a bad smell, just earthy like trees and grass and mud, undercut by the salty musk of sweat. She struggled to concentrate.

"All right," she said.

"What you want to do is squeeze the last bit out of the trigger just as it drifts across. Just try to relax. Breathe in, breathe out, breathe in and hold it."

Listening to his voice in her ear, Jolie did as he instructed. The crosshairs did not move so wildly now, and she let them touch the post as she squeezed off the last fraction of tension in the trigger. The rifle fired and instantaneously through the scope she saw a chunk go flying out of the post.

"Oh!"

"Ain't so hard, is it?" Cole said. "They say women are the best shots anyhow, on account of their center of gravity being lower than a man's. All I know is you just shot the shit out of that fence post. Now, see if you can do it again."

Jolie fired several more shots. The last three hit

the post. When she turned to look at Cole, he was standing a few feet away, smiling with satisfaction.

"Not bad?" she asked.

"Not bad."

"I want to be a good shot. That soldier you captured told me where the sniper Von Stenger is staying in the chateau. I know just where it is. I am going there tonight to kill him. He has killed enough Frenchmen and Americans." She didn't know why she had told him.

"All right."

Jolie gave him a look. "You are not going to try and stop me?"

"Darlin', back home in the mountains, revenge is a way of life. People polish up revenge and treasure it like a pretty stone. I reckon you've about had it with being kicked around by these Jerries. Fair enough. I just don't think you've got much of a chance against the likes of him with that rifle and I doubt you can just walk into that chateau carrying a Mauser with a scope on it. You might need something more sneaky like."

"Like what?"

He stooped and pulled a wicked-looking little knife from his boot. "If I was you, I'd get in close and stab that son of a bitch in the belly with this here pig-sticker. He might take a while to die, but you'll kill him sure as shit."

She took the knife. "Thank you. And Cole—I like that name— please do not tell the lieutenant. He might not understand. I agree that he is one who plays by the rules."

"Like I said, Jolie, what rules? This here is a war."

CHAPTER NINETEEN

THE SHOOTING LESSON OVER, the remaining band of snipers packed up and moved out. Lieutenant Mulholland had no clear orders other than to engage the enemy, and so they trudged along the road toward Carentan. The action at the bridge had taken up most of the long June day and already the shadows stretched far and deep across the fields.

After the rush of adrenalin and pounding hearts during the fight, they now felt curiously empty, like a balloon that the helium had gone out of.

It wasn't a feeling that lasted long. They had not gone far when they were overtaken by a Jeep tearing down the dirt road. It was a little unusual to see one of the Jeeps traveling alone. Considering that the woods and fields all around them were still contested by the Allies and Germans, the occupant would have been better off in a Sherman tank or even on foot. The sharp whine of the Jeep engine attracted too much attention. Whoever was at the wheel had to be either desperate or foolish. The vehicle skidded to a stop beside them.

"Ya'll are snipers?" the sergeant at the wheel asked. With the dark circles under his eyes and unshaven face, he had the haggard look of a man who hadn't slept in a while. His eyes went to the tele-scopic sights of their rifles, and he didn't wait for an answer to his own question. "You could maybe do some good up this road at a little town called Bienville. We took it from the Germans today but they chewed us up good. There's only about a hundred men holding the town, and it looks like the Germans will try to take it back tomorrow."

"Seems to me like you're going in the wrong direction," Mulholland said. "If they're so hard up for help, why are you heading away?"

"We only had two radios and they're both shot to hell. I volunteered to drive out and try to get us some reinforcements."

"We could hear that Jeep coming for miles. You're quite a target," Mulholland said. "You'd be better off on foot, or even on a bicycle."

"No time for that," the soldier said. His foot toyed with the clutch and the Jeep lurched forward, rolled back. "We need to hold that town when the

Jerries show up in the morning. It's one of the key points along that road into Carentan. I think we took them by surprise, but if we give up that town we'll lose twice as many men getting it back."

"Right up this road?" Mulholland asked. "It looks like we're headed that way. Might as well see if we can help out."

"Shoot a Jerry for me," the driver said, and let his foot off the clutch. The Jeep shot forward and careened down the road between the tall hedges.

Lieutenant Mulholland turned to look at his squad. His command now consisted of two snipers (or maybe one and a half considering Vaccaro probably couldn't hit a target smaller than a barn), a French girl, a captured German boy and an English paratrooper so gung ho that the lieutenant suspected the Tommy had maybe landed on his head coming down. Somewhere along the line they had become a seriously motley unit. All they needed now was for a stray dog to tag along.

"Jesus," he said out loud to no one in particular. He didn't normally use the lord's name lightly but that was par for the course since coming ashore at Omaha Beach; he was beginning to question what sort of person he had become over the last few days. Nobody had prepared him for this at OCS.

The little group stood in the road, waiting for him to tell them what to do. Getting antsy, Vaccaro shifted his rifle to his other hand and spoke up, "Lieutenant?"

At times like this, the lieutenant sometimes thought of his grandfather, who had served with General Grant during the Civil War. He recalled a family story about his grandfather saving the famous general from a Confederate sharpshooter. Had Brendan Mulholland ever felt this overwhelmed? It had been a different time and a different enemy, but the lieutenant took strength from the fact that he wasn't the first Mulholland to fight a war. His grandfather hadn't let General Grant down, and Mulholland wasn't about to give up on his ragtag squad.

"You heard the man," Mulholland said. "Let's go rescue us a town."

* * *

THE TOWN of Bienville was a deceptively quaint and sleepy French village. With its old stone houses, shops with brightly painted signs and doors, church steeple, and narrow cobblestoned streets, the village was the sort of place a traveler on the road to Carentan might have used up a frame or two on a precious roll of film to capture.

Indeed, the town thrived mainly on commerce because it was surrounded by wet, boggy marshes that did not make good crop or grazing land. To make matters worse, the Germans had flooded the marshes to ensnare paratroopers. The flooded fields and marshes around Bienville now held the drowned bodies of scores of American paratroopers.

The flooding also had created a bottleneck so that anyone bound for the key Norman city of Carentan had to stay on the road through Bienville. Skirting the town through the flooded fields surrounding it would be impossible. Beyond the marshes were the hedgerows to contend with. Essentially, the Germans had managed to make the village into a key strategic point. Nobody was getting anywhere by road in Normandy unless they came through Bienville.

And yet the Germans had lost the village in a short, sharp battle the day before. The invasion at the beaches had caused such confusion that the German High Command in Normandy had overlooked the defense of the town. The small force in the village had been taken by surprise when a unit of Americans suddenly came up the road and raced into town.

The German defenders fled or were killed; a Wehrmacht doctor and several medics had stayed behind to care for the wounded on both sides, turning the church into a makeshift hospital. There was no hope yet of transporting the wounded back to the beach head for more advanced medical care.

No stranger to conflict, the village had grown up

around the church founded in the eleventh century. Other troops had marched through; other battles had been fought nearby. Though this was a French village, the combatants were now Germans and Americans, and the weapons were rifles and machine guns rather than spears and broadswords, longbows and crossbows.

The old stone walls were pockmarked by bullets. In the narrow streets between the buildings, the smell of cordite mingled with the scent of fresh-baked bread.

The American defenders had set up a machine gun nest overlooking the main road into town, which the snipers approached cautiously.

"Hold your fire!" Mulholland shouted, then waved. Somebody waved back, and they approached the town.

"Don't tell me you're the freakin' cavalry," one of the machine gunners said. "We're gonna need a few more guns to hold off the Germans if they send Panzers at us."

"Hey, buddy, we can turn around and leave if you don't want us," Vaccaro said.

"Don't get sore," the machine gunner said. "We'll take what we can get. We've only got about eighty men to defend this place. How many do you think the Germans are going to send at us in the morning?"

"More than eighty," Vaccaro said.

"Yeah, it's like Custer's Last Stand all over again," the machine gunner said. "Lucky for us the Jerries don't take scalps."

The snipers moved into the village itself. Everywhere they looked, the American troops were scrambling to set up defensive positions, using wooden carts, even mattresses and tables to create firing positions at the street corners. Some were busy rigging so-called "sticky bombs" to use against the Panzers that would surely be there by morning. A few soldiers occupied second or third floor windows, getting ready with grenade launchers. The thick stone walls made each house a fortress in its own right.

Mulholland reported to the captain in charge, who agreed that the snipers should be placed wherever Mulholland thought best.

"All right, listen up, here's our plan," Lieutenant Mulholland said. "Neville, I want you to position yourself and your Tommy gun in one of the upstairs windows near the edge of the town. That will add some firepower to what's already covering the road into the village. The Germans will likely be coming out of the south, so Vaccaro, you get yourself up on one of the rooftops. The higher up, the better, because you'll have a longer field of fire. You start trying to pick off Germans as soon as they come into sight. Cole and I will go up into the church tower, which is the highest point in the village."

"What about me?" Jolie asked.

"There's a hospital set up in the church," he said. "Maybe you and Fritz can help."

They made their way over to the church, which was by far the largest structure in the village. The massive stonework and squat architecture gave the church a brooding appearance, and the square gray tower at one end of the church resembled a castle keep more than a steeple.

The church doors were open, and they started inside, but were stopped by a young man wearing a red and white medic armband. His uniform was spattered with blood. "No guns in the church," he said. "This is neutral territory, sir."

"All right," Mulholland said. "I can't argue with that. It is a church, after all."

"Thank you, sir."

They left their weapons behind and the young medic led them inside. After the bright light of the French countryside, it took a while for their eyes to adjust to the dark interior, lit only by the sunlight through the tall, narrow windows that were little more than slits in the deep stone walls. The air was cool, and smelled of rubbing alcohol and unwashed bodies. The pews were being used as hospital beds, and in many places blood had soaked into the ancient wood. It soon became apparent that Germans and Americans were among the wounded. Mulholland

looked around, and saw that several of the other
medics—marked by their white arm bands with
medical crosses—were Germans.

"You've got Jerries in here?"

"Yes, sir. Our own boys and Jerries, along with a
couple of French civilians who got caught in the
crossfire. I guess technically the Germans are prisoners of war, but we've called a truce to help the
wounded. You know, I was their prisoner at first
because my parachute came down almost in the
middle of the town, when the Germans still had
control of it. They treated me all right. One of these
Germans is a doctor, and he really knows what he's
doing. There would be a lot more dead without him."

"Word has it that the Germans might try to take
back this town in the morning," Mulholland said. He
nodded at the massive double doors that opened
toward the steps leading into the church tower.
"Defensive positions are being set up outside. I want
to set up a sniping post in the church steeple."

"Sir, you're an officer, so I suppose I can't tell you
what to do, but the fact is that if you start shooting
from that steeple, the Jerries are going to hit back,
maybe with mortars, maybe with Tiger tanks. They'll
turn this place into rubble. With all due respect, sir,
is that really what you want with all these wounded
men in here?"

Mulholland took a moment to look around the

interior of the church. Fritz moved among the wounded, speaking with them in German. The German doctor heard him, waved him over, and set him to work helping bandage a leg. Jolie kneeled beside a girl, no more than eight or nine, who lay wounded on one of the church pews.

"I suppose you're right," Mulholland said. "I'll leave the woman and the German with you. That's two extra pairs of hands."

"Thank you, sir."

Mulholland turned to Cole. "OK, there's a lot of hours between now and dawn. Get something to eat, get some sleep, and then we'll get into position before sunrise. Obviously, the church steeple is now off limits, so we'll have to find ourselves a roof top."

"I reckon there's plenty of roof tops," Cole said. He smiled. "Plenty of Jerries to shoot, too, once that sun comes up."

* * *

JOLIE WAITED UNTIL DARK, then stole a bicycle and peddled toward the chateau that now served as Wehrmacht headquarters. At first, she tried to be stealthy, but that seemed ridiculous to attempt on a bicycle when every rut and pot hole sent the machine rattling like a bucket of bolts.

It was hard to tell if she was riding through territory held by the Germans or by the Americans—at night, with trigger happy and exhausted soldiers everywhere, running into troops from either side would be equally dangerous.

If anyone stopped her, she planned to pose as a French girl on a desperate errand—a sick relative perhaps. The Americans might stop her, but the Germans would be more wary. With luck, any German sentries she came across wouldn't shoot her.

Fortunately, the small lanes she kept to were deserted except for the occasional owl, fox or rabbit.

Jolie knew these roads well. She had grown up in Normandy, of course, but it was her role in the French Resistance that had truly taught her the best routes to travel the bocage by night, undiscovered.

The Allied invasion had been long awaited by Jolie and the other French *maquis*. She recalled the grim days of June 1940 when the Germans had arrived. She had watched in disbelief as the truck-loads of German troops drove in with their square steel helmets and harsh, guttural orders. German was truly a soldier's language.

Many French had accepted the Germans with a grudging shrug. For the most part, the Germans were easy to get along with—unless you happened to be a Jew. All of the Jews in Normandy were quickly rounded up, never to be seen again.

There were some French, like Jolie, who would

not give up so easily—at least not in their hearts. This became the French Resistance and she had quickly joined. There had been nighttime raids on supply trains and radio centers. Small groups of soldiers traveling at night might not reach their destination.

But the Germans made the French pay dearly for these acts of rebellion and the *maquis* soon limited operations to gathering intelligence for the Allied invasion to come. They bided their time.

Jolie's first real lover was a young Resistance fighter named Charles. He was tall and had dark, Gallic good looks. He took terrible chances on missions, yet he was shy in bed. She still recalled the feel of his skin against hers—there was no better feeling in the world.

He was captured one night while counting gun batteries at the beach. The Germans shot him in the courtyard of the very chateau she was riding toward tonight.

Jolie had gone with some women of the village to collect the body. She never cried for Charles. They both knew what they were doing was dangerous, and Charles had paid the ultimate price.

Thinking about Charles, Jolie peddled harder, until her heart raced. She was beyond tears for her handsome lover, dead at the hands of the German occupiers. What Jolie craved now was revenge.

CHAPTER TWENTY

AFTER ESCAPING THE WOODS, toward nightfall Von Stenger returned to the chateau in hopes of some food and rest. In the room that he had shared with Wulf and the boy, there were now three enlisted men. They lounged on the battered furniture, resting their muddy boots on the upholstered chairs. He mused that one didn't need bombs to destroy buildings, just soldiers.

"Get out," Von Stenger said.

The men were unshaven, battle-hardened veterans and they might have argued, considering that his rank insignia was hidden beneath his camouflage smock, but they took one look at the scoped rifle, the Knight's Cross at Von Stenger's throat and the cold blue eyes, then cleared out.

"Ich habe über der sniper," he overheard one of the

men say out in the hallway. *"Dieser Mann ist ein kalt-blütiger Killer."* That man is a cold-blooded killer. *"Ich mag es nicht sniper. Das Gespenst."*

He looked around the room, which now felt very empty. Wulf was dead and the boy was either captured or dead. He did not mind being alone; in fact, he preferred his own company.

The enlisted men had lit a fire in the old fireplace. Von Stenger took off his boots and his camouflage smock, then put them by the fire to dry. His belly rumbled. Even *Das Gespenst* got hungry. He wished he could order up room service. He smiled to himself. Room service. Wouldn't that be something! That might be the perfect war, he thought, if one could hunt the enemy by day and then return to one's hotel to a good meal.

Well, perhaps he could do something about that. He went out into the hallway in his stockings and found a fresh-faced orderly who was properly intimi-dated by the sight of a Wehrmacht captain, and sent him down to the kitchen with orders to bring him a plate of food.

There was an air of excitement throughout the old chateau. Like Von Stenger, many of the men here were resting for the night before getting back into action at daybreak. Though battle weary, no one showed any indications of being defeated. While the Allies had landed in force—Americans, Canadians,

Scottish and English—the Germans had far from lost the fight. Reinforcements were pouring in, including SS units and Panzer divisions, all under the command of General Rommel. The Allied air superiority combined with the sheer numbers of enemy troops might push the Germans out of Normandy, but they would make them pay for every acre between the hedgerows.

The Allies were learning what war meant—it was the kind of war some of these German troops had been fighting for years. They were professional soldiers who were good at killing, Von Stenger included. No one bore any particular grudge against these invaders—it wasn't as if they were fighting the hated Red Army—but they were simply the enemy.

The crowd at the chateau included a few women, most of them tearful. These were French women who had cast their lot with the occupiers—out of love or the advantages that having a German lover brought. Now that the Germans might be leaving, they were fearful. There would be repercussions—shaved heads, drumming out of town—that consorting with the enemy would bring. Frantically, they were either looking for their men who were now dead or somewhere in the field. Some of the unluckiest ones now had bastard babies fathered by German soldiers.

Everywhere, Von Stenger heard stories being traded about exploits that had taken place earlier that day. He lit a cigarette and lounged in the hallway and listened.

"You should see how the Tiger tanks make short work of the Sherman tanks being used by the Americans and Tommies," one soldier said. "One shot and that is it for them. *Kaboom!*"

Another soldier was talking about the battle at Bienville, a village on the road to Carentan. Von Stenger was well aware that Carentan was one of the larger towns on Normandy's Cotentin Peninsula and the Allies were eager to capture it, but first they had to collect the little towns that dotted the road like beads on a string. Bienville was one such place and there had been a hot skirmish fought there that day.

"We were the last ones out," the soldier said. He had a bloody bandage wrapped around his upper arm. "We found ourselves trapped in the church and so we planned to make a last stand there. We would have been captured or killed, I suppose, but the priest showed us a tunnel that led out into the marshes. He said there had been enough bloodshed for one day. We had to leave our wounded behind. The Americans are holding Bienville now, but we are taking it back in the morning."

The orderly reappeared with a plate of food. The plate was piled high with steak, potatoes and red cabbage. There was a tall mug of black coffee. Von Stenger was impressed. It was more than he could eat. He had the orderly bring it to his room. If this had been a hotel, Von Stenger would have given him a tip. But one did not tip soldiers. Instead, he gave him half a bar of chocolate. The orderly was still young enough that his face lit up at the sight of the candy. "Thank you, *Herr Hauptmann*!"

Von Stenger pulled a chair and a small table close to the fire and had just sat down when the orderly returned.

"*Herr Hauptmann*, there is someone downstairs to see you."

"Who?"

"A woman." The young orderly blushed a bit. "She asked for you by name."

Von Stenger was puzzled as well as curious. He was certain that he did not know a single woman in France, so who could it be? "Well, bring her up."

He took out his Walther P38, set it on the table beside the plate, and put a newspaper on top of it. The orderly appeared in the doorway, followed by a French woman Von Stenger did not recognize. He guessed that she was in her early twenties, and she was good looking rather than pretty. She wore trousers, which was in itself unusual, and an unflattering sweater the color of old dead leaves; her hair was pulled back in a business-like bun and she wasn't wearing any makeup. The dark eyes that glanced at him were wary and sly, like those of a fox. This was no simple local girl. One of the *maquis*, he thought. French Resistance. He stood out of politeness as she entered, but as he did so he kept one hand on the table beside the newspaper.

"Hello *mademoiselle*," he said in French, bowing politely but keeping his eyes on her. "I do not believe we have met. To what do I owe the pleasure?"

The young woman hesitated, and her hand drifted to the small of her back, just where she would keep a knife or pistol. His hand edged closer to the hidden Walther. Then the woman dropped her hand.

"You are Von Stenger? I have information for you."

"In that case, you are just in time for supper." He told the orderly to drag an empty chair up to the table. He would have done it himself but he did not want to turn his back on this woman. "Please, have a seat."

"Really, I must—"

"Join me," he said. "I insist. I hope you have not come to tell me that we have a bastard child together, like these poor wretches in the hall. What will you French do to them once we have gone?"

"Once you have gone?"

"*Mademoiselle*, the Allies have landed thousands of troops and scores of tanks. They control the skies. It is a foregone conclusion that we cannot hold Normandy. The numbers are not in our favor.

But we shall make them pay dearly for it. Please, join me."

The woman sat, and the orderly was back in a minute with an empty plate for her, as well as a knife and fork. She stared, somewhat wide-eyed, at the steak and potatoes. The French had to make do with less wholesome fare, while the best food went to the occupiers.

"That smells delicious," she said, and slowly, as if against her better judgment, she reached for her knife and fork.

"The spoils of war," he said. Von Stenger considered a moment, and then asked the orderly to bring him the bottle of Bordeaux that he had been keeping in his rucksack, wrapped carefully in a rag. "I have been saving this for a special occasion. I have the feeling that tonight may be my last opportunity to enjoy it."

"Why do you say that?"

"Please, let us enjoy this food and a glass of wine, and then we shall discuss whatever it is you have to tell me."

The orderly produced two dusty water glasses that were none too clean, but Von Stenger supposed the alcohol in the wine would neutralize anything harmful. He then made sure the orderly found a third glass, which Von Stenger filled for the orderly before sending him into the hall.

"I did not realize that German officers were waited upon in this fashion," she said.

He chuckled. "Rank has its privileges in the Wehrmacht. We don't always have it so good, you know. I nearly lost my toes in Russia. Of course, you French are no strangers to the finer things. Might I remind you that we are in a chateau that was built in the seventeenth century as home to a baron. We should be grateful to him. Come now, enjoy your meal."

They ate in silence for several minutes. Von Stenger thought the wine was particularly good with the steak. The orderly had left the bottle on the table, and he poured himself a second glass. They both must have been hungrier than they thought, for soon all that was left on their plates were a few scraps of fat and potato skins.

Von Stenger pushed his chair back from the table. "Now, what have you come to tell me?"

"In the morning, you Germans are planning to attack Bienville and take back the village, which is now held by the Americans."

"Are we?" Von Stenger sipped some wine. "Hmm. That is quite delicious, wouldn't you agree? If only we had some cheese to enjoy with it. Now, I don't wish to be rude, *mademoiselle*, but usually when one is an informant it is customary to supply information about what the *enemy* is planning."

"There is only a small force of Americans holding the town at the moment, but they have been reinforced by several snipers."

"There are snipers everywhere in the bocage."

"One of these snipers has a Confederate flag on his helmet. Some of his comrades call him the Johnny Reb Sniper. He is, by far, the best sniper in Normandy. He likes to say that he can shoot the eye out of a flying bird."

"That would be fine shooting," Von Stenger agreed. "But I have to respectfully take exception to him being the best sniper in Normandy. You see, that would be me."

"I have heard you are called The Ghost."

"It is a name I came by in Russia. The Eastern Front. Compared to Normandy, you might wonder why anyone would fight over that place."

"Did you shoot many Russians?" she asked with a disgusted tone.

"As many as I could. More wine, *mademoiselle?*"

The French woman stood, her hand going again to the small of her back. He could see that she was shaking, and Von Stenger had been fighting long enough that he recognized it as the kind of tremor that overcame someone when they were about to do something foolish and brave.

Von Stenger thought that the time for subtlety had passed, and he tossed the newspaper aside to reveal the pistol. "Please," he said. "Let us not do anything that will give us indigestion."

The woman's eyes widened, and she let her hand drop. "Now you know," she said. "This Johnny Reb Sniper will be at Bienville in the morning. The question is, will you?"

"I look forward to seeing him in my crosshairs." Von Stenger smiled. "And then we shall see who is the best shot."

With that, the woman turned and left. It took him a moment to realize that he had just been challenged to a duel.

CHAPTER TWENTY-ONE

JOLIE SLIPPED BACK through the American lines and returned to where the snipers had set up camp in the courtyard of an old house. She wasn't ready yet to face Cole and give him back his knife. She wasn't sure how she would explain to him that she had failed to kill the German sharpshooter.

Instead, she decided to report to Lieutenant Mulholland. He had dragged an old chair into the garden shed and was using an upended wooden pail as a desk as he went over a map of Normandy.

His M1 rifle was propped nearby. It was a semi-automatic, perhaps not as accurate as the Springfield, but it could send more lead in the enemy's direction, in less time. The higher rate of fire was an advantage if one wasn't such a crack shot, and the lieutenant had no illusions about his abilities with a rifle, despite the fact that he commanded a counter sniper squad.

Mulholland's face lit up at the sight of Jolie, but his expression soon changed when she explained where she had been and what she had learned. She had expected him to be grateful for the information. Instead, he slapped the top of the makeshift table in anger.

"I can't believe what I'm hearing," the lieutenant said. "You went to see the Germans? What the hell were you thinking?"

"We needed information," Jolie explained. "That is how we *maquis* find out what the Germans are up to. We go talk to them."

"It was a stupid thing to do," Mulholland said. "You could have been captured."

Jolie blinked in surprise. The French Resistance had been successful by being daring and taking chances. It was the only real weapon they had against the occupying Germans. "Do not lecture me, Lieutenant. I have been fighting the Germans for four years. You yourself have been fighting them for four days. It stands to reason that I know what I am doing, *n'cest pas?*"

"I hate to point this out to you, *mademoiselle*, but after four years the Germans are still here. Your tactics may take some revision."

"Are you going to ask me what I found out, or are

you more interested in insulting me and my countrymen?"

"All right then, what did you find out?"

"I did not go to see just any German," Jolie clarified. "The boy we captured, Fritz, told me where the German sniper was staying. His name is Captain Von Stenger, and he is the best sniper the Germans have in Normandy. He has fought in Russia, and Spain before that. He was even an instructor at the German's sniper school." She recalled Von Stenger's cold blue eyes and good manners. "He is from the upper classes. I would say he likes the finer things. Good food, good wine. I know because I had supper with him in front of the fire at a chateau about five miles from here. We had steak and potatoes and wine, and were waited upon."

The lieutenant's jaw dropped. "You ate with this sniper? Excuse my French, but holy shit."

"What is French? I think you mean *merde*."

"Never mind. Did you find out anything useful, or did you just get a good meal out of him?"

Jolie took her time answering, studying the lieutenant before she spoke. He was not a bad-looking man, and under the stubble and grime and fatigue she could see that he was still a very young man. Command did not seem to come easily to him, and his earlier anger appeared to be out of genuine concern for her safety.

When she had first laid eyes on him she had thought *hmm*. In a war, it was dangerous to think about romance or anything but surviving that day and the next. Her love affair with Charles had taught her that much. But someday the war would be over, *n'est-ce pas?*

Her thoughts then drifted to Cole. He was a rough, hard man, savage and almost feral, so very different from the lieutenant. He had more in common with the really vicious Resistance fighters—perhaps even with the ruthless SS men—than he did with the other Americans. She thought again—Cole? *Hmm*—then pushed that thought away and focused on the unhappy lieutenant.

"I set a trap for him," she said. "I told him that your sniper unit is in Bienville. Here in this town. I told him that Cole is the best sniper in the American Army, and that Cole is here."

"You did *what?* Why on God's Green Earth would you sic that German sniper on us by telling him we were here?"

"Lieutenant, if you saw this man you would know he is not the second best at anything. He considers himself to be *the* best. He knows Cole is good. Cole is responsible for killing two of his comrades, who were very good snipers themselves—he shot one and outfoxed the other so that Meacham could shoot him. I made certain he knew Cole was to blame. Cole has almost shot this Ghost Sniper. Almost. And so, he will come to kill Cole. He won't be able to help himself. He will come here. And then we will shoot him."

The lieutenant shook his head. "What you have done is stupid and dangerous, *mademoiselle*. I don't see how luring Von Stenger here is a good idea."

"He will be here," Jolie said. "Von Stenger verified that the Germans will be making a push in the morning to take back the town. Von Stenger will come with them when they show up. You see, we have to stop him. You saw how many men he killed by himself. One man with a rifle. It is your duty to stop him."

"My duty, huh?" The lieutenant nodded. "You may be right about that, *mademoiselle*, but I don't agree with your methods. And tomorrow, when the shooting starts, I want you inside the church. You are not to fight. We need you as a guide. You have risked enough. Understand me?"

"I am not one of your soldiers to be ordered about," she said.

"You're right that you are not a soldier," the lieutenant said. "Like I said, you stay in the church, out of harm's way."

Jolie nodded, though she had no intention of obeying. "Of course," she said. "You are the boss."

* * *

LATER THAT NIGHT, Cole was cleaning his rifle when Jolie found him in the kitchen of an abandoned house on the main street. Wisely, most of the town's residents had fled for the countryside. He had disassembled the Springfield and had the parts spread across a blanket on the kitchen table. She watched him rub down the bolt action with solvent. Then he began running a cleaning rod through the barrel.

"I could not do it," she said. "I could not kill him."

"Don't fret on it," he told her without looking up, still busy cleaning the rifle. "Killing someone is an ugly business. Sounds a whole lot easier to do than it is, no matter how much you might want to do it."

"He had a pistol, like he suspected something. If I had tried to stab him he would have shot me."

"Then this Ghost Sniper ain't a fool. Give him that much. And he didn't shoot you when he could have, just to be ornery, so I reckon that's something in your favor."

"He was playing with me, like a cat with a mouse." She shook her head angrily. She took out the knife Cole had given her and tossed in on the table, where it landed with a clunk. "I should have taken that out and stuck it straight into his heart! *Merde!* But I could not."

"You not being able to kill him just means you ain't a monster like he is."

"What about you? You have killed other men."

"In case you ain't noticed, Jolie, there's a war on. Pretty much anyone who ain't dead by now has killed someone here in Normandy."

"You killed men before the war."

He looked at her sharply with those cut-glass eyes. "How would you know that?"

"It is a way you have about you. You are afraid of nothing. When you look at someone, it is like you see right through them."

Cole didn't answer for a long time. "You ain't like me, Jolie. You ever seen a wolf or a panther? No, ain't likely here in France now, but maybe back in the old days your grandpa saw one. Well, I've seen them back in the mountains. They are pure wildness. Ain't many of them left, and some people say they're all gone, but I seen 'em. They are hunters, Jolie. They hunt down other animals and kill them. Ain't nothin' cruel in a wolf or panther when it kills, no right or wrong, good or bad. *Predator* is the word for it. They're hunters, born to kill. It's how God made 'em. Let's just say I've got a lot of wolf or panther in me. It's how God made me. You think that's how a person should be? No, you're the normal one, Jolie."

Jolie was a little surprised by the speech—it was certainly the most words she had heard Cole speak at one time. She had the disconcerting realization that she had felt the same presence when talking with the German sniper. So he was a wolf or a panther too. A hunter. "Von Stenger will be here in the morning," she said. "He will try to kill you."

"Then he won't be the first to try it," Cole said. "And don't forget that we'll be trying to kill *him*. That's why you invited him to the hoedown. Now, give me that rifle of yours and let's give it a cleaning."

Cole had already reassembled the Springfield, and now he set it aside and laid the rifle taken from the dead German sniper on the table. "Mauser K98. One thing about these Germans is that they make good equipment. Good planes, good tanks, good rifles. All I can say is we are damn lucky we're fighting 'em now, after the Russians done worn them down. We're mostly fighting older men and boys. Good thing, too, or they would have tossed our asses right back into the ocean."

Expertly, even though he had never done it before, he disassembled the German rifle and set the parts on the blanket: bolt, stripper clip, scope. Then he dabbed some solvent on a clean rag and began to rub down the bolt action, almost lovingly, removing tiny metal filings and powder residue. When he finished, the metal gleamed.

"Lieutenant Mulholland was not happy with me for going to see Von Stenger."

"You told him?" Cole shook his head. "The lieutenant ain't a bad man, Jolie, but he's a man who follows the rules, which don't include sneaking behind enemy lines and meeting with the Jerries. Besides, I've seen how the lieutenant looks at you like you were a piece of French pastry. Maybe a slice of chocolate cake. Mmm. Mmm."

Jolie laughed. "You are joking!"

"He was worried about you."

"Were you worried about me?"

"Hell no. I've heard all about you French *maquis*. Resistance fighters. You're too tough to worry about."

"So you do not see me as a piece of chocolate cake?"

"Nope. You look more like stale French bread to me. Or maybe an old baked potato with a leathery skin. Like I said, you're tough."

"You know how to flatter a girl!" From the crinkles at the corners of his eyes, she could tell that he was teasing her. She could not help but smile. Then her smile faded as Jolie thought again about how she had not been able to bring herself to stab the German sniper. He would be out there, waiting for them, waiting for Cole, in the morning. "Maybe some of us are not as tough as you think."

Cole started on the rifle barrel next, threading a cotton patch soaked in solvent onto the cleaning rod. He entered the barrel from the action end, following the path that a bullet would take through the barrel. The Mauser was a slightly different diameter from the Springfield and the rod going into the barrel was a tight fit. He eased the tip in, then worked the rod through until the patch emerged at the muzzle, showing streaks of black where it had reached deep into the contours of the rifled grooves.

Jolie watched him work over the rifle and then finally put the Mauser back together, thinking that he was wasting all that attention on a weapon. *Hmm*. When he was done, she reached across the table and took his hand.

"What?" he asked.

"Tomorrow may be our last day. I want a good memory to take to my grave."

She led him into one of the bedrooms upstairs. Neither of them spoke a word. She unbuttoned her blouse, took his hand, and placed it on her breast.

"You call yourself a lone wolf," she said. "Show me how a wolf makes love."

Jolie stepped out of her trousers, revealing milky white legs. Cole had heard rumors that the French girls didn't shave, but her legs were a smooth alabaster. She guided his hand between her legs. Cole's fingers opened her up and Jolie moaned happily at the realization that he had done this before. This was not the night for virgins. She fumbled for his belt and shoved his fatigues down.

They did not bother to undress all the way. He laid her across the bed and Jolie hooked one leg around him, resting her foot at the small of his back. It was a good thing they were alone in the house because the headboard was soon banging rhythmically against the walls. A framed picture shook loose and fell, but they ignored it.

Noise carried far in the almost deserted town, so Jolie took his fist and put it in her mouth, biting down as a shudder ran through her. When they had both finished, they lay tangled together for several moments, hearts pounding, breath jagged.

Cole noticed the broken picture frame on the floor. He figured the French owners would suppose a bomb had shaken it off the wall; he had to smile at what they would think if they knew the real reason—and what had happened on their bed while they were hiding in the bocage.

Cole rolled over and held her, but there was nothing possessive in his embrace. His lean arms were corded with muscle; Jolie was sure he could have crushed her if he had chosen to.

She wondered how it would have been to have made love to the lieutenant. His body would have been softer, his touch gentler. He would have felt guilty; he would have apologized. He might have proposed marriage. Cole just stroked her contentedly without saying a word. For a night such as this she had chosen the right man.

They lay there for several minutes, catching their breath. Then the sounds of a countryside at war began to drift in—the distant chatter of machine gun fire, and much closer, in the streets below, the noise of soldiers shouting to each other as they readied their defenses for the German assault that was sure to come at dawn.

Jolie slapped his bare ass and pushed him off, though she was smiling as she did it. "I have heard from the other French girls that you Americans do not have much technique. You make love like you were storming a beach all over again," she said. "Still, you are not bad for a wolf."

He shook his hand painfully. Her teeth had left a semi-circle of tiny bruises across his knuckles and a fleck of blood showed where the skin was broken. "Damn, but you French girls have got a bite."

Jolie smiled. "Maybe there is a little panther in me, after all."

AFTER THE FRENCH GIRL LEFT, Von Stenger sat for a long time smoking, looking into the fire, and finishing the wine. It was, quite clearly, a trap. The *maquis* hated the Germans; the girl had not given him the information for any other reason than to make sure he would be at Bienville in the morning. Once there, of course, she planned for the American sniper to kill him.

Von Stenger wondered about the American. From what he had seen, this hillbilly sniper was a good shot, and he was too clever by far. He would be some backwoods person, a skilled hunter, a deadly marksman. He would have little education, but enormous cunning. He knew this kind of sniper because he had faced them before, in Stalingrad. And he had shot them. Because while they were talented, most of the Russian snipers were not trained. There were methods and tactics they knew by instinct, but not in the textbook way that Von Stenger knew them. Training beat instinct every time—or almost every time.

Like the Russians, the American would have had very little real training as a sniper. The American had come to play a deadly game of checkers, but what Von Stenger had in mind was a game of chess.

The first rule of sniping was to keep one's enemy off balance by doing the unexpected. Von Stenger planned to take part in the attack on the village, but not in the way that the French *maquis* or the American marksman expected.

He finished his cigarette and flicked it into the

fireplace, then went out into the hall where soldiers slept along the old stone walls.

It took him a while, but finally Von Stenger found the man whom he had overheard talking about his escape that day from Bienville. The soldier was sharing a bottle of schnapps with a comrade, and both of them appeared well on their way to being drunk.

"You there," Von Stenger said, and the man blinked up at him in surprise. "Tell me about this tunnel you used to escape from the church today."

CHAPTER TWENTY-TWO

IT TOOK a pot of strong black coffee to sober up the soldier, who sat at a table in the bustling kitchen of the chateau while Von Stenger packed himself some food. Von Stenger put together a ham sandwich, an apple, and a flask of coffee.

The soldier was reluctant to go out into the night. "The *maquis* are everywhere in the bocage country," the soldier said. "They would like nothing better than to cut our throats."

"You can take your chances with the *maquis*, or I will shoot you now for disobeying an order," Von Stenger said nonchalantly. The look in his eyes, however, was more than convincing. "If you are lucky, the *maquis* won't ever see you, but I won't miss."

The soldier did not say much after that, but led him down a road toward Bienville. The soldier was something of a clumsy oaf—noisy as he was, he was probably justified in being worried about the French Resistance—but he tried to follow Von Stenger's example of moving almost silently along the road.

The towering hedges at the sides of the road pressed against them like a vise of blackness. Normally, Von Stenger would have carried his rifle slung over one shoulder, but he kept it at the ready, his finger on the trigger. At every step, he expected to be ambushed by the *maquis* or the Americans, or possibly shot at mistakenly by German troops.

Something skittered in the brush and his rifle flicked toward the noise. Von Stenger caught a flash of liquid blue eyes in the starlight. Feral eyes. He looked more closely at the still, dark form on the ground nearby. The animal was feeding on a corpse.

"What is that?" the soldier whispered, sounding close to panic.

"Just a fox," Von Stenger replied. "You see, it must be a good night to be prowling the countryside."

The hedges fell away as they entered the marsh country around Bienville, and soon the lights of the village came into view. It was not a bright night, but there was just enough light to pick out the roof tops and church tower against the lighter backdrop of the French sky. Von Stenger sensed that they were now surrounded by water.

"The marshes were flooded to make it harder on

the enemy paratroopers," the soldier said. "I saw them coming down in this mess. The water isn't deep, maybe up to chest height. A lot of them drowned when their harnesses and gear pulled them under."

"Shut up," Von Stenger whispered. "We are almost close enough for them to hear us in the village."

Over the centuries, the road had been built up into a kind of causeway above the marshes, so that it wouldn't flood when the nearby rivers occasionally overflowed their banks. It was good they were crossing the causeway under cover of darkness; by day they would be an easy target.

"Here," the soldier said. "I think this is the place. We need to move off the road."

They couldn't risk showing a light, and so had to grope their way through the dark. The ground here was swampy rather than flooded, covered in thick clumps of marsh grass and stunted shrubs that tore at their clothing.

Von Stenger muttered a curse as he stumbled for the third time. The mud sucked at his boots and water seeped in, getting his feet wet. "Idiot! Where is this tunnel?"

"It is nearby, sir! I know it is!"

"The sooner you find it, the sooner you can get back to your schnapps."

But it soon became clear that the soldier was doing little more than stumbling around in the dark. They nearly tripped over an old wooden skiff pulled up on the bank. Von Stenger was worried; all that one of them needed to do was fall and make a splash, and that would alert the Americans. They were within machine gun range of the village now and if the Americans heard a noise, their guns would cut Von Stenger and his guide to pieces.

"I do not understand," the soldier muttered. "I know it was nearby. It was—"

"Right here," Von Stenger said. They had come to a place where the land sloped abruptly and the flooded expanse lapped at their feet. Cut into the side of the bank was a hole lined with stone, almost like a well shaft turned on its side.

"We have found it," the soldier said, greatly relieved.

"Get out of here and try to do it quietly," Von Stenger warned. "The Americans will be listening for any sound."

"Aren't you coming back?" the soldier sounded surprised.

"No, why would I do that? You have shown me the tunnel into the village. Now I am going to pay the Americans a visit."

Von Stenger had not brought his pack, but only the rifle, spare ammunition, a few stick grenades, the

food and coffee, canteen, and a flashlight. He had
removed any insignia that might catch the sunlight or
starlight.

The opening of the tunnel was no more than one
meter high. Even as he waited to see if the soldier
would make it back to the road without bringing
attention to himself, the water of the marsh had risen
so that it now flowed into the mouth of the tunnel.
He realized that the dammed-up rivers were tidal,
and the tide was coming in quickly.

When he judged that enough time had passed for
the soldier to have reached the road undetected, Von
Stenger moved deeper into the tunnel. It was like
moving into the pit of night itself. He switched on
the flashlight—it wouldn't be noticed now that he
was deeper in the tunnel—and saw that the walls
were very wet. Perhaps high tide covered the tunnel
entrance? Well, that would make things interesting if
that was the case.

It was hard to say who had built the tunnel, or for
what purpose. He had heard that some churches in
Germany had similar tunnels—they had been used
only recently in some cases to hide Jews or smuggle
them to safety. Churches had a history that involved
centuries of intrigue. The tunnel could have been
built by a scheming priest, a smuggler, or a nobleman
who needed a quick escape in times of political trouble. No matter—it surely had served someone well in

times past. Von Stenger would now use it for his own ends.

The tunnel was roughly built, with the flashlight beam revealing where several loose stones were missing so that the earth spilled in. In more than a few places, roots had burst through and formed a tangle that he narrowly squeezed past.

It was a wonder that the whole thing had not collapsed at some point. Von Stenger was careful to avoid bumping the sides and sending the whole thing crashing down around his ears. The old bricks were slick with moss or slime, but the tunnel itself was curiously free of vermin, though he detected the odor of mice.

From the tunnel entrance to the church he judged it was not more than one hundred meters—not terribly far, unless one happened to be crawling on your hands and knees, encumbered with a rifle, and trying to navigate by the feeble light of a battery-powered torch. In other words, it felt like kilometers to Von Stenger. It seemed to take forever.

But it was Von Stenger's plan, and he stuck with it. As Goethe had said: "Thinking is easy, acting is difficult, and to put one's thoughts into action is the most difficult thing in the world." He mused that Goethe would not have imagined this maxim being applied to the action of crawling through a tunnel toward a sniper's nest.

Finally, he sensed a draft and the air smelled fresher. The dull beam of the battery-powered torch revealed a wooden ladder coming down from above. The ladder looked rickety with dry rot. A couple of the rungs showed signs of being freshly broken—that would have been from the soldiers coming down.

Von Stenger reached up, took hold of a rung—and promptly felt it snap in his grip. He tried again, reaching higher, and this time the wood held. Gingerly, he put his foot on a rung, keeping his weight toward the edge of the ladder rather than the center.

One rung at a time, he climbed until he reached the underside of a trap door. Keeping one hand on the ladder, he pushed against the trap door. Nothing happened.

He fought a momentary sense of panic—what if the trap door was hidden beneath something heavy, like a chest? He reached up again, using two hands, and felt the trap door lift a few inches.

Struggling mightily—the damn thing was heavy and he felt as if he were lifting the gravity of the earth itself—the trap door budged enough for him to open it a few inches. He realized it was not hinged, but only a loose panel set into the floor. He shifted it, heaving against the weight, until he had moved the panel enough for him to crawl through.

He pulled himself out of the tunnel and lay on the

floor, panting with the effort. He found himself in a kind of hallway with a staircase and realized he was at the base of the church tower. Double doors opened up into the church itself, which he saw had been converted into a hospital. He was surprised to see both American and German uniforms among the medics as well as the wounded scattered on the church pews.

No one had noticed him yet. They were all far too caught up in the hubbub of treating the wounded. As nonchalantly as possible, Von Stenger got to his feet, walked over to the double doors, and swung them shut. He dropped an old-fashioned cross bar into iron slots to bolt the door shut. There was so much thick oak in the doors that he was sure it would take a battering ram—or perhaps a Panzer—to break through. Those doors were the only way into the tower.

He started up the stairs. The ancient stone steps were worn smooth and he climbed them silently, keeping the rifle ready in case there was already a sniper in position up there. But the tower proved to be empty. Through the narrow window slits, he had a commanding view of the town below, and by moving from one window to another, he could cover all approaches to the church. The stone walls were so thick that it was like being inside a fortress.

Von Stenger drank some coffee and smoked a

cigarette, relaxing, waiting for it to get light. The spring night was cool and damp, and despite the thousands of troops scattered across the countryside, the night was strangely quiet. In the distance, he heard the hoot of a hunting owl, then the bark of a fox. Night sounds. It was such lovely countryside here, and so close to the sea.

Gradually the light began to come up in the East, and with it came the swell of birdsong. The birds were soon drowned out by the whir of approaching engines. Those would be the Panzers coming down the road toward town. Below him, in the fading night, he began to pick out shapes moving along the streets. Now it begins, he thought.

He was the ghost. *Das Gespenst.* He had haunted the forests of Spain and the ruins of Stalingrad, bringing death one bullet at a time. And now he had come to this little French town.

He sighted through the scope, which gathered the faint light, and settled the crosshairs on a soldier hurrying to occupy one of the makeshift defenses at the edge of town. His finger took up the last of the tension in the trigger and the soldier crumpled into a heap.

The second battle for Bienville had begun.

CHAPTER TWENTY-THREE

"HERE THEY COME!" a soldier shouted.

Cole was sprawled on a second-floor roof, looking down the road, his eye pressed to the rifle scope as he awaited the first glimpse of the enemy.

No one really needed to shout a warning. They had been able to hear the engines and clanking treads of the approaching Tiger tanks for some time, a sound that was as threatening as a distant thunderstorm. There would be ground troops, too.

Let them come on, he thought.

He wondered just where Von Stenger might be. Was he with the advancing Wehrmacht troops? Made up of marsh and water, the countryside surrounding the town did not offer the hiding places of other areas in the bocage. The woods and fields the German sniper could use for cover were at an extreme rifle range. Nonetheless, Cole knew Von Stenger was out there somewhere. Jolie had practically dared—or perhaps a better word was taunted—the German sniper into being there. But where?

He reckoned that Von Stenger hadn't earned the nickname The Ghost without good reason.

Cole had chosen his sniping position with Von Stenger in mind. It was up high enough to give him the advantage because the shooter with the higher position held all the cards. He would have preferred to be up in the church steeple, which with its height and thick walls would be impregnable. It looked more like a castle or knight's keep than a church steeple. Lieutenant Mulholland had agreed with the medics that the church should be neutral territory as a makeshift hospital.

He was using the ridge of the roof as a rifle rest so that the slope of the roof gave him some natural protection. All he had to do was keep his head down once the shooting started.

And it was about to start.

It was hard to say how long the beleaguered American force could hold this key town on the road to Carentan. Their best hope would be for reinforcements—or better yet a squadron of P-51 tank busters to magically appear and knock out the Panzers. For now, they would have to depend upon themselves. They were well dug in, and that combined with the fact that the attacking Germans would be channeled down the single roadway into town, gave them a defensible position. The Germans' superior numbers and firepower might eventually wear down the Americans, but they would go down fighting.

Neville, the lone Brit, was on the second floor at the edge of town with his Tommy gun, while Vaccaro, the lieutenant and Cole had taken up positions on the roof tops of the highest buildings. Jolie and Fritz were in the hospital.

Cole was a little surprised when he heard the sharp crack of a rifle in town and thought someone was getting antsy, firing before the enemy was even in sight. But then he noticed the crumpled figure in the street below, looking as if he'd been shot. *Huh.* Cole might have ignored that if a second rifle shot hadn't rung out, the bullet knocking down another soldier. That second shot had definitely come from within town limits, and it had killed a soldier.

What the hell was happening?

A third shot rang out, and Cole was fairly certain it had come from the church tower. The tower was much higher up and directly behind him—he was lucky that it was still dark enough that the sniper couldn't see him yet.

"Sniper!" he heard someone shouting. "There's a sniper in the steeple!"

It had to be Von Stenger. The Ghost Sniper. No

doubt about it. Jolie had thought she was setting a trap for the German, but the sneaky son of a bitch had turned the tables. Somehow, the bastard had slipped into the town. He had gotten into the church steeple. And now he was picking them off.

On the narrow streets below, men shouted and pointed up at the tower. From one of the slitted windows, Cole saw a stab of flame. *There*. He aimed and fired, too fast, not thinking through what he was doing. He knew the bullet was wrong before it left the barrel. His hasty shot blew a chunk of rock of the edge of a window slit. The bullet had missed, but it had gotten the Ghost Sniper's attention. Cole could feel himself in the crosshairs. He flung himself over the ridge of the roof just in time—a bullet pulverized the tiles where he had lain a split second ago.

Damn good shot, he thought in the back of his mind. His next thought was: *I'm a dead man if I don't get off the roof.*

With the German in the church steeple above him, there was nowhere safe to be on the roof, though the ridge of the roof itself offered some protection. *Keep moving, Cole.* He rolled and a bullet nicked the roof tiles near where his head had been a moment before, blasting Cole's face with shards of slate.

Move. Now.

Cole had climbed up carefully because the ancient

roof slates were brittle and slippery with what someone might have described poetically as moss, but which was really more like the algae you found on rocks near the edges of slow-moving creeks.

He knew he had seconds before the next shot killed him. There was only one way to get down, and that was fast. He scrambled toward the edge of the roof, gaining momentum until he was moving feet first across the slick slates like a kid down a snow bank. He tossed his rifle free, catching a glimpse of it pin wheeling into thin air, then tried to catch the edge of the roof to slow himself down. If all went well he could hang down off a gutter and his feet would be six feet closer to the ground.

It didn't work that way. His hands missed the gutter and he felt his belly lurch sickeningly as he dropped like a wing-shot bird toward the ground.

Helpless, he fell.

He hit the top of a truck parked below, then bounced off and landed on the hood. His next stop was the cobblestoned street, where he landed so hard that it knocked the breath clean out of him. He had a scary few seconds trying to get his lungs working again. Then his breath came back in a gush.

He was out of sight of the German sniper now, so he took his time getting up and taking stock. Nothing broken, but he hurt like hell. Cole glanced up at the roof, which seemed very high above where he sat, aching and bleeding, on the cobblestoned street.

He reckoned he was damn lucky that some French farmer had left his battered truck parked beside the house, though the roof of the cab was more like a metal slab than a feather bed. Still, it had broken his fall somewhat. Otherwise, he would have landed right on the cobblestones and burst open like a watermelon.

Cole looked around for his rifle. He found it a few feet away, and his heart sank at the sight of it. The stock was cracked, the scope busted. He picked it up and a little shower of broken glass tinkled down on the cobblestones like frozen tear drops. *Christ on a cross.* Here he was with a sniper lording it over town and half the German army on its way, and him without a goddamn rifle. *Don't it just figure.* Maybe he could throw rocks at the son of a bitch.

"Have you lost something?"

The French voice came out of the shadows, and he was still disoriented. He spun around, trying to locate the source. Then Jolie materialized as she stepped out from behind the truck.

"Busted my rifle, and damn near busted my ass permanently," Cole said. "By the way, I reckon that's your sniper friend up in the church tower."

"He is not *mon ami*." She reached out a hand and helped him up. "Are you all right?"

"Darlin', I done fell off a roof. How the hell do you think I am?"

"It seems like a reasonable question."

"Well, I reckon I'd be a lot worse with a bullet in me. How the hell did he get up there?"

Jolie shrugged. "He is the Ghost Sniper."

Cole did not care to admit it, but he was shaken by far more than the fall from the roof. Jolie had made sure this so-called Ghost Sniper would come to Bienville by practically handing him a party invitation. All things being equal, Cole would have had a good chance of eliminating someone who had been a deadly killer of their own troops. But the German had beat them at their own game.

Cole did not like to be outfoxed, and that was just what the German sniper had done. Now the other sniper had the high ground, the upper hand, and here was Cole cut and bruised with his rifle busted. As a matter of fact, he was getting worked up about it. *Gettin' goddamn mad.* He took a deep breath. Gettin' mad got you killed. He knew what he had to do was get even.

"Here, take my rifle," Jolie said. "You are much better with it than I am."

"Jolie, them Germans movin' toward town ain't here to play patty cake. You best be able to shoot back."

"I hate to say it, Cole, but there are many GIs

who won't be using their weapons anymore. I will take one of those."

Cole nodded, and she handed him the rifle she had used for her shooting lesson. It was the Mauser K98 they had taken off the dead German sniper who had been hidden in the forest. He knew it was a good rifle—probably superior to the Springfield. It had a nice heft to it and the scope was better than the American one had been. Say what you wanted to about the Germans, but those bastards knew how to make good rifles and good optics.

She passed over several clips of ammunition. While there weren't enough rounds to get the average G.I. through a brief fire fight, it was more than enough for a sniper. Cole had only one target in mind. He needed just one bullet for that.

He glanced up at the church steeple. Another shot rang out, and somewhere in the town another American died. *I'm comin' for you, you son of a bitch.*

CHAPTER TWENTY-FOUR

Up in the church steeple, Von Stenger watched the American sniper tumble off the roof and he sent a final bullet after him like a kick in the pants, hoping for a lucky hit.

Was the sniper wounded? He knew at least one of his bullets had come close. If nothing else, the American sniper was going to have a painful landing and perhaps a few broken bones. It was hard to know the man's fate because the other sniper had fallen off the far edge of the roof, so that the house itself blocked his view.

At any rate, he would not be hearing from the American anytime soon—and he was the only enemy sniper Von Stenger really had to worry about.

He felt a vague sense of disappointment because he had welcomed a challenge, or something akin to a duel. The French girl had clearly summoned him to Bienville in hopes that the American sniper would put an end to him. However, he had outwitted them because the last thing anyone expected was for him to appear in their midst.

Shot after shot, he now continued to wreak havoc in the streets below. The Americans darted from building to building in confusion. It was a little like watching ants scramble. Out of sheer frustration, one of the American soldiers fired a rifle grenade at the tower, but it only bounced off the thick stone walls and detonated mid-air with an ear-splitting blast, scattering shrapnel through the streets. Someone cried out in agony.

As the morning light grew brighter, Von Stenger concentrated his fire on the makeshift barricade the Americans had erected at the edge of Bienville. Although the barricade was equipped with a .50 caliber machine gun, the Americans' hasty efforts at defense were almost laughable. The barricade consisted of a wooden cart turned on its side, a few old wine casks filled with earth, even some bales of straw, in hopes that they might deflect a bullet. That was wishful thinking. He supposed the barricade might help them hold off infantry, but there would be Panzers as well, and the tanks would make short work of the defenders.

As soon as he picked someone off, another soldier

scrambled to get behind the .50 caliber machine gun. The deadly weapon had been facing down the road, ready to cut down the advancing Germans, but now they were trying to get it turned around to fire on the church tower. Von Stenger wasn't about to let them. Thick as the stone walls were, he didn't wish to test them against the heavy slugs of the machine gun.

Two more soldiers worked to reposition the gun. He shot one, worked the bolt action of the Mosin-Nagant, and then shot the second man, who slumped forward over the gun itself. *Eins, zwei, drei* ... there were now half a dozen bodies around the machine gun emplacement, but who was counting?

A few shots peppered the walls of the tower, but Von Stenger had been careful not to present himself as a target by staying well back from the slit windows. He was positioned very nearly in the center of the tower.

One bullet did pass through the slit and bounced around inside the bell chamber like a fat, very angry bumblebee trapped in a jar. The noise made his blood run cold. The bullet finally spent itself and Von Stenger breathed again. He always had been lucky, but knew better than to push that luck.

It would only be a matter of time before the Americans found someone who could shoot well enough to put shot after shot through the slit window ... and one of those zipping bullets would give him a fatal sting. He planned to be long gone before that happened.

He emptied his next-to-last clip at the soldiers scurrying below. He thought he had brought enough ammunition, but was quickly running low. It was all a little too much like being at a pheasant shoot, where the helpless birds were released before the so-called hunters, where they were quickly gunned down.

Von Stenger knew he could not stay up in the tower forever. The massive doors that closed off the entrance to the steeple steps from the main nave of the church itself were made of ancient oak, more like iron than wood. The doors were heavily barred—all a hold-over from the violent medieval era when most buildings were constructed with defense from attack in mind. The French priests had not been fools.

Of course, a few explosives or a heavy machine gun would turn the oak doors to splinters. But the interior of the church was now a hospital, filled with badly wounded men who were not easily moved. The Americans would think twice before trying to blast through the doors. The only alternative was to chop through them by hand.

Targets were getting harder to find, so he took a break from shooting to light a cigarette. He would let the Americans think that the pause in his shooting meant that he had been killed by some lucky stray shot. That would draw them out.

* * *

Lieutenant Mulholland gathered a group of men to make a run at the church where the sniper was hidden in the tower. From his earlier visit to the church, he knew that oak doors led toward the stairs into the tower. Breaking them down would not be easy, but he and his men had rounded up a few axes, a pry bar, and even a couple of garden mattocks. Basically, they had collected anything that they could use to chop at the doors.

"Vaccaro, you and Cole cover us," he said.

"Don't worry, Lieutenant, we'll give that Nazi some lead to chew on," Vaccaro said.

Jolie came running up and took a position next to Cole, armed with an M1. Mulholland knew that he had ordered her to stay in the church to help the wounded, not fight.

"What are you doing here?"

"I am fighting."

"Like hell you are!"

"I may be a woman, Lieutenant, but I am not much of a nurse," she said. "I am much more useful with a rifle."

Mulholland would have argued, but there wasn't time. "Have it your way," he said. He nodded at Vaccaro and Cole, and the two snipers aimed their rifles at the slit windows in the church tower. "The rest of you, let's go!"

They ran straight for the church. Mulholland could see that it would be impossible for the sniper to shoot almost straight down at them, so the faster they got to the church, the better their chances would be.

Behind him, Vaccaro and Cole fired a few quick shots at the tower to make sure the sniper kept his head down.

Mulholland sprinted for the church. *We're gonna make it, we're gonna make it—*

He hadn't counted on the grenades.

UP IN THE TOWER, Von Stenger spotted the group of soldiers running toward the church with axes and crowbars. He had to smile. The sight of these men armed like peasants reminded him of the movie *Frankenstein* that he had seen in Berlin. Von Stenger did not care much for movies, but that one had been amusing.

He did not smile for long. The men were quick as rats, and they darted through the streets toward the church before Von Stenger could get a good shot at them. They charged toward the entrance to the church.

The narrow slits of the church tower made it awkward to shoot straight down, but Von Stenger had anticipated this situation by bringing along four stick grenades. He unscrewed the "bottle-cap" base and tugged the ceramic bead that ignited the five and a half second fuse, then dropped it out the window above the doorway below. He quickly followed it with a second grenade.

Even up in the tower, he felt the shock wave of the double blast. The screams below told him that the grenades had been effective.

CHAPTER TWENTY-FIVE

THE BLASTS CAME in rapid succession, knocking Mulholland down and literally filling his mouth with dirt as he skidded belly first across the ground. He heard men screaming and wondered how badly he was hurt.

He rolled over, his ears ringing from the concussion. To his surprise, he seemed to be in one piece. He'd heard before that the German stick grenades were mostly about the flash and bang—not nearly so deadly as the American "pineapple" grenades. However, it was clear to Mulholland that the German grenades were more than effective. Two men were on the ground now, writhing in pain. One of them had an ugly leg wound, the torn flesh looking like raw steak. Mulholland crawled the last few feet into the stone doorway of the church, and the other survivors followed.

Fritz, who was now one of several surrendered Germans working in the makeshift hospital, rushed forward to help Mulholland to his feet.

"I'm OK, I'm OK," he said, shoving Fritz toward the door. "Do something for those poor bastards out there."

The medic and the German doctor who had appointed themselves in charge of the church hospital confronted him. "No weapons in the church, Lieutenant!" the medic said. "The Jerry doc and I agreed that this is neutral ground."

"In case you haven't noticed, there's a Jerry sniper up in the steeple. Now get the hell out of my way, unless you want me to shove this ax up your ass sideways."

They rushed up the aisle past the pews filled with wounded Germans, Americans and French civilians toward the oak doors at the back of the church, to one side of the altar. He gave one a shove with his shoulder, but it didn't budge.

"Barred shut from the inside, goddamnit! All right, boys, get chopping!"

* * *

Von Stenger heard the gunfire increasing in town and thought that his ploy with the stick grenades had drawn the Americans' ire. But no additional shots seemed to be striking the tower.

Keeping well back from the windows, he looked down the road leading toward town. The view from the church tower was really quite spectacular, and now that the sun was properly up he could see for miles. The sunlight sparkled across the flooded fields and revealed the miles of rich green bocage country beyond that. It was shaping up to be a lovely June day. Coming up the road was a Tiger tank flanked by a unit of advancing infantry. To a German soldier, that was a sight even more lovely than the French countryside. Out in the open, however, the Wehrmacht infantry was exposed and the American fire even at that extreme range was having a telling effect. There would be some empty rooms at the old chateau tonight.

Then the infantry fell back and the Tiger rolled forward alone. Its massive turret gun fired, sending a shell screaming toward town. The shell whistled past the church tower and landed among the houses at the far end of town. The high explosive round detonated, flattening several dwellings into rubble.

Von Stenger was far less worried about Americans armed with axes chopping through the oak doors than he was concerned about his own side's tanks.

Their assumption would be that the church tower was occupied by the Americans or by American observers keeping an eye on German movements. The Tiger tank would be targeting the church tower, and the tank gunners were highly trained and notoriously accurate. They would soon have the range worked out.

Time to go.

He went down the cold, stone stairs, taking his time. When he reached the base of the tower, he heard the dull thud of an ax hitting the oak doors. So his stick grenades had not gotten everyone. No matter. By the time they chopped through those doors, he would be long gone.

The trap door was still open. It had been covered over by an old rug, which now lay crumpled to one side. Von Stenger thought about that, shut the trap door, and dragged the rug over it. It would take someone that much longer to discover the door under the rug. Lifting one side, he got the edge of the trap door open and shimmied under it. The door was very heavy, and it was only with great effort, muscles straining, that he was able to hold it up enough to slip under. The effort was worth it. Standing on the rickety ladder in the tunnel itself, he lowered the trap door so that the rug would now cover it again once the trap door was shut.

He descended the ladder carefully—the brittle

wood threatened to collapse under his weight. Then he was down on the tunnel floor, crouched over. He clicked on his battery-powered torch and made his way back toward the tunnel entrance in the marsh.

He was surprised to find that water was sloshing under his hands and knees and getting deeper as he crawled forward. What on earth? He could see the tunnel entrance up ahead, a bright hole in the darkness, and moved toward it, but something was wrong —the tunnel exit wasn't nearly as bright as it should be in full daylight. Puzzled, he stared ahead and realized what it was. The tunnel entrance was nearly under water.

Von Stenger crawled faster. Perhaps it was only his imagination, but the water seemed to be rising by the minute. The approaching high tide, along with the spring flood itself, was soon going to fill the opening of the tunnel with water. But there remained a gap between the surface of the water and the roof of the tunnel entrance. Holding his rifle high, above the water line, he took a deep breath and pushed through the last few feet of the tunnel.

Fully prepared to swim for his life, he bobbed up in the flooded marsh. As he got his feet under him, he realized with relief that the water in the flooded field was no more than waist high or chest deep at the most, even now with the approach of high tide. Of course, in the tunnel one was forced to go along on hands and knees, so the flood there could drown you.

He had brought along a length of rubber tubing to use as a breathing tube in case he had to slip under the water to escape, but there was no one around to see him, so he simply waded out into the flooded fields.

Soon, the Americans would find the tunnel entrance in the church. They would want revenge for the blood he had spilled. They would be coming after him. Von Stenger would be ready when they did.

One hundred meters out he spotted an island of sorts in the flood—a clump of trees and brush encircled by the flood waters. It was perfect for what he had in mind. Eventually, his plan was to rejoin the German forces once they had recaptured Bienville. Until then he would hide in the flooded fields and marshes.

As he waded toward the island, careful to keep his Mosin-Nagant out of the flood waters, he bumped into something that floated just beneath the surface. He used his knee to push it out of the way, but the submerged object shifted and rolled, and he had a terrible start when the thing bobbed up to reveal a human face.

"Scheisse!" he shouted, and jumped back, ready to defend himself.

But the face was pale and bloated, the blue eyes

blank. He saw that the corpse wore the uniform of an American paratrooper and that the body was still entangled in parachute cords. The dead man was outfitted with a steel helmet, an M1 strapped across his chest, and a fully loaded haversack. Von Stenger surmised that the poor bastard had become tangled in his parachute lines, then was dragged under by the weight of his gear and drowned. This fate was exactly what the Germans had intended by flooding the marshes and fields in the Allied drop zone. For this soldier, the trap had worked all too well.

He contemplated the body for a moment, then nodded to himself.

Von Stenger drew his combat knife. Working quickly, he cut the drowned man free of the parachute cords and haversack. Then he dragged the body along behind him and continued on his way toward the island.

"Come along, *Ami*," Von Stenger mused aloud to the corpse. "You and I are going to be good friends."

CHAPTER TWENTY-SIX

WOOD CHIPS WERE STILL FLYING when Cole came running up with Jolie and Vaccaro. He watched the lieutenant swinging his ax like a mad lumberjack. The oak doors shuddered under each blow but still did not budge.

"Who would have thought the son of a bitch had grenades," Vaccaro said. "He's a sniper, for crissake. But I think maybe I got him."

"Nobody got him," Cole said. "I reckon he's still up there waiting for us."

"In that case, you go first."

"You know, for a city boy, you ain't so dumb as you look."

The axes opened a jagged hole through the door. Someone shoved a pry bar through and got it under the crossbar, but it took three men and some cursing to shift the weight enough to get the doors open.

Cole was the first one through, his rifle at the ready. The room at the base of the tower was no more than fifteen feet on each side, and empty. Although it was bright daylight outside, the interior was chill and shrouded in semi-darkness because the only light came from the few window slits cut into the ancient stone walls.

"Anybody bring a flashlight?" the lieutenant asked.

"No, but I eat a lot of carrots," Cole said, and started up the stairs. Mulholland started to pass him, still carrying the ax, but Cole stopped him with a wave of his hand. "Are you goin' to throw that there ax at him? I got this, Lieutenant."

From a few steps behind, Vaccaro bellowed up the stairway. The words echoed and carried like smoke up a chimney: "We're comin' to get you, you goddamn sneaky Nazi sniper son of a bitch! How do you like that, huh!"

Cole looked down and fixed him with a pale stare. "Vaccaro, what I just said about you bein' smarter than you look? Well, you ain't. If he didn't hear them axes, you just sent him a telegram that we're on our way up the stairs."

There was no helping that now, so Cole continued up the ancient steps, worn smooth by centuries of priests going up to ring the bell and summon the faithful to mass.

It would be easy enough for the enemy sniper to ambush them from any of the landings above, but that would have to happen at very close quarters, exposing himself to return fire. If Cole had been the German, and he'd had any more stick grenades, he'd bounce them down the steps. If he had a crate of grenades, the sniper could defend himself up in that steeple until he died of old age. But Cole doubted he had lugged that many up there.

No sense worrying about it. With his finger on the trigger of the rifle, he forced himself up another step, and another. Soon, he could see the rectangular opening into the belfry itself. Cole slung his rifle and drew a .45 automatic, then crept silently up the last few steps.

Back when he was a boy, Cole used to hunt wood-chucks. They were animals that resembled a beaver but that dug burrows from which they poked their noses, sniffing for predators.

He had often seen how a fox would wait patiently beside the hole for a woodchuck to put its nose out and provide dinner. Hunting them, Cole had learned the same technique. All you needed to shoot a wood-chuck was a nose and maybe an eye showing.

If Cole stuck his nose above the floor level, he was fairly certain he would get shot. So he stuck the

.45 up instead and sprayed shots in several directions. The noise was deafening. He surged up the steps and into the belfry, both hands on the gun, ready to fire.

Nobody there.

He was soon followed by Mulholland, Vaccaro and Jolie. "He really is the Ghost Sniper," Jolie said.

"He was here, all right," Cole said. He had noticed a gold-trimmed cigarette butt on the stone floor. With his boot, he toed at an empty shell casing. The Cyrillic markings were just visible. "Our sniper shoots a Russian rifle. It was him."

"He didn't just vanish," the lieutenant said. "He could be hiding."

They made a quick inspection of the tower room. The windows were too narrow to crawl out. There was no attic to hide in. Down below, the oak doors had been barred shut from inside—which meant the sniper hadn't slipped out at the last instant just ahead of them.

"Huh," Cole said.

Vaccaro, still panting from the climb, looked around the empty room. "Hillbilly, I know you're a man of few words, so let me say them for you: Where the hell did he go?"

Cole lingered at one of the slit windows long enough to see the advancing German column. There were an awful lot of Germans heading for Bienville. However, they were forced to stay on the road because of the flooded fields surrounding the town and roadside.

If he could have stayed up in the tower, there was no telling how many he could pick off. Then the Tiger tank fired and a shell whistled close by the tower. If their aim got better, the tower would not be standing much longer.

He started back down the stairs.

"Cole, where are you going?" Mulholland demanded.

"Well, sir, he ain't up here."

They descended quickly, not worrying about an ambush on the stairs this time. But the room below was as empty as ever, with a bare stone floor. The only furnishing was a tattered rug on the floor.

"Did you expect to find that Jerry down here making coffee or something?" Vaccaro asked.

Cole looked at the rug more closely, saw that one corner was flipped up. He reached down and tugged at the rug, revealing the trap door set into the stone floor.

"I'll be damned."

The trap door was awfully heavy, and it helped to have two men to swing it all the way open. A shaft led down into a dark tunnel that smelled of dank, musty earth. Over Cole's shoulder, Vaccaro lit a wooden match and dropped it down the shaft. The sputtering flame revealed the ladder and tunnel below, but no sign of the enemy sniper.

"I'm going after him," Cole said.

"Huh," Vaccaro said.

* * *

NOBODY HAD A FLASHLIGHT, so Vaccaro gave Cole his Zippo lighter.

"Hey, I want that back, so don't get shot."

"I'll see what I can do about that."

Cole went down the ladder and then stood on the floor of the shaft. He could see the others looking down at him, including Jolie—she had not done very well in following the lieutenant's orders to stay out of harm's way.

"I will meet you at the other end," she said.

"Where's that?" Cole asked.

"It must come out in the marsh," she said. "The priests would have wanted a way to reach the river without being seen."

"I wish we had known about this goddamn tunnel before now," Cole said.

Jolie shrugged. "France is full of secrets."

"Cole, you are one crazy mountain man," Vaccaro said, peering down from above.

Lieutenant Mulholland spoke up. "I won't order

you to go after that German," the lieutenant said. "But I won't tell you not to."

"In that case I reckon I'm going to nail that son of a bitch's hide to a barn door," Cole replied.

He had to get down on his hands and knees to enter the tunnel. He flicked the Zippo to get his bearings. The roof and sides of the tunnel were shored up with damp bricks and ancient boards that looked punky with rot. It smelled like an old root cellar. He peered into the darkness that pressed up against the dim light from the flame. The tunnel seemed to go on and on. How long was it and where did it lead? The flickering lighter flame did not reveal much beyond a few feet ahead.

It was awkward trying to crawl forward on his hands and knees while juggling the rifle and a burning lighter. He snapped the lighter shut and was immediately enveloped in darkness. He kept one hand wrapped around the rifle, keeping it more or less pointed ahead of him and ready to fire. He pushed on into the tunnel, less worried about where he was going than by the thought that the Ghost Sniper might be somewhere just ahead, waiting to ambush him.

Cole was totally helpless in the tunnel—there was no way that the German could miss if he suddenly opened fire. Briefly, Cole considered firing a few shots into the darkness ahead in case the German was up there, but decided against it. If the German didn't know he was being followed, Cole would only be tipping his own hand.

Don't give nothin' away. Whoever had the element of surprise held all the cards.

He crept deeper into the tunnel. The dim light from the trap door faded until it was like crawling through a blacksnake's belly.

While the floor of the tunnel felt damp to the touch, the crumbling ceiling was powder dry, so that when his head accidentally brushed the bricks over-head, bits of dirt and mortar rained down. Judging by the debris in his path, someone had recently been this way. He moved ahead blindly, feeling the tunnel seem to press in around him.

Then came a rumbling sound and Cole was enveloped in choking dust. He crawled faster, knowing without seeing it that part of the roof was coming down. *Faster, faster.* Bricks bounced off his shoulders, but he managed to outpace the crumbling ceiling. The sound he heard was much like a shovelful of dirt hitting the bottom of a hole—that *whump* sound—only a whole lot louder.

He stopped panting, and half turned in the cramped tunnel to light the Zippo.

"Christ on a cross," he muttered.

It didn't look good. The lighter flame was tiny, but in the depths of the tunnel the flickering light was bright as an explosion, revealing the fact that a good portion of the tunnel had collapsed behind him.

No turning back now. There was only one way out, and that was forward. He felt that his chances of running into the German were slim now, so he took his knife and cut a strip of cloth from the tail of his uniform shirt and wrapped it around the Mauser's muzzle to keep the mud out. Then Cole kept going.

His hand touched water, and soon he was making his way across a wet, slippery floor. The water grew deeper as he moved ahead, rising around his wrists, his knees, his shoulders. He slung his rifle across his back.

For the first time since entering the tunnel, he stopped.

Water. Why did it have to be water?

His thoughts went back to the day he had almost drowned in Gashey's Creek while trapping beaver. He had been under a long time, all tangled up in rope and the submerged branches of drowned trees. By all rights he should have died. Feeling the water all around him now and the same blackness, Cole fought back a momentary panic as the darkness seemed to take on weight and viscosity like some tangible thing —oil or a heavy wet blanket. He felt it close in around him and the cold water felt like it was squeezing his chest. He found it difficult to breathe and his heart raced. Even now, the water seemed to be rising. Every fiber of his being screamed *get out, get out, get out*.

The German sniper had come this way. Cole was sure of it, and he was going after him no matter what.

But where the hell had the German gone? *There.* Up ahead, barely visible in the distance, Cole could see that the tunnel brightened. He understood now that he was looking at the only way out.

The flooded river and marsh covered the tunnel entrance. He could see that the tunnel angled sharply up from the entrance and that the water covered the entrance much in the same way that water fills the bottom of a tilted glass.

If Cole held his breath and swam—hard—he might just make it out.

More chunks of the ceiling pattered down on his helmet like rain on a tin roof. *Ping. Ping.* Then bigger chunks of brick. *Pang!* The whole goddamn roof felt about ready to collapse and there was nowhere to go.

Swim or die.

Cole made sure the rifle sling was secure across his back, took a deep breath, and dove.

The water was cold, cold and black, and he imagined something like dead hands reaching for him to pull him under for good. He kicked wildly and flailed his arms, trying to propel himself forward but mainly managing to skin his knees and elbows in the process. Cole ignored the pain. He swam toward the light. His lungs burned. Just a few more feet. His rifle stock got hung up, catching on a loose brick. He paused long enough to wrench it free. The effort meant a few precious bubbles of air escaped his lungs.

Almost there. He shoved forward—and then he was outside the tunnel, about to come up for air.

Mixed with relief was a question—where was the German?

Cole hovered for a moment beneath the surface. The water was not all that deep—definitely not over his head. He got his feet under him. His lungs ached, every molecule in his body wanted air, but he would not let himself come up just yet. He unstrapped his helmet, then holding it by the bottom rim lifted it above the surface, while simultaneously pushing his face out of the water, just enough to get a breath.

Then Cole dove again.

He was just in time. He felt the helmet nearly plucked from his grasp with terrible force. With his eyes open under the water, he saw a bullet leave a contrail through the water.

He swam as long and as far as he could, his lungs burning again, but at least this time he wasn't in that goddamn black tunnel.

Another bullet streaked down where his helmet had been. He was already several feet away.

He picked out a log floating above him and popped up behind it, keeping his head down. Peeking from behind the log, he could make out a small island a couple hundred feet distant. If he were the German sniper, and he'd had time to choose his position, that's just where he would be, ready to pick off whoever came out of that tunnel.

Missed me, you son of a bitch. Now it's my turn.

CHAPTER TWENTY-SEVEN

Von Stenger saw a helmet decorated with a Confederate flag clear the water. He fired. The helmet sank, a black hole in its center where the round had punched through. He fired again into the water just where the sinking body should be.

The natural inclination was to think *that's that* and call it a day, but Von Stenger did not move except to work the bolt action. Then he settled down to wait.

He had a strong shooting position there on the island. While the river lay in the distance, the dammed waters had flooded the marshes and fields, forming a tremendous shallow lake that spread for hundreds of acres around Bienville and beyond. The water was filled with the flotsam and jetsam lifted by the flooding—logs, fence posts, mats of straw.

The sun was at his back and the sparkling glare

across the water gave anyone approaching from the raised roadway—or the sunken tunnel entrance, for that matter—a distinct disadvantage in having to squint into the diamonds of sunlight reflected on the water's surface.

Von Stenger was using the dead body of the American paratrooper as a decoy. Partially hidden and in the prone position, with a rifle grasped in its bloated fingers, the corpse appeared to be lying in wait on the island. Von Stenger himself was hidden in the brush several feet behind the corpse, hoping that another shooter—half blinded by the sun-dappled waters—would think the body was actually the sniper. With the enemy's crosshairs elsewhere, Von Stenger could then pick him off.

He believed that there was just one man who would have made the effort to track him through the tunnel. The hillbilly sniper. The distinctive flag on the helmet was proof. Von Stenger realized that he had missed killing the man on the roof top.

By all appearances, he had been more successful this time in killing him. He had certainly hit the American sniper's helmet. But some gut instinct told Von Stenger to hold back.

It helped to be a good shot, but the first rule a sniper learned was patience.

And so he waited.

* * *

COLE WONDERED if the rifle would fire, after getting a good dunking. Fortunately, he had thought to wrap the muzzle with a strip of cloth. That kept out the mud. The water would drain out. The cartridges were water tight. But if the scope had water in it, he was out of luck.

Carefully, working behind the shelter of the floating log, he lifted the rifle parallel to the water and took off the cloth. He opened the action to drain any water, but was surprised to find it dry. So far, so good. Finally, he put his eye to the telescopic sight. The seal had held—not a drop had penetrated the scope. Not for the first time, he was amazed by the quality of what the Germans made. An American scope would be junk by now.

The floating log had a kind of knobby fork in it, and Cole rested the rifle there, trying hard not to move the log too much. *Easy, easy.* He now had a good view of the island where the German sniper must be hidden.

Then he saw him. Partially obscured in the brush he could make out the outline of a helmet. He grinned. Cole settled the crosshairs on the helmet and gently squeezed the trigger.

* * *

THE DEAD PARATROOPER'S body shuddered as the bullet struck it. Von Stenger saw that the shot must have come from the log floating near the tunnel entrance. He did not have a clear view of the American. Instead, he aimed for the water just in front of the log and fired, hoping a lucky shot might hit the enemy sniper.

A bullet lost most of its energy almost immediately upon hitting the water. It was like shooting into wet concrete. But all he needed was a few inches.

Other than the splash where the bullet had gone in, there was no movement. A body slumping under the water would have caused enough displacement to move the log. So he had missed.

The American sniper must now have realized that the body he had shot was nothing but a decoy. Now he would be looking for the actual shooter. Von Stenger, however, was confident that he was well hidden.

In spite of the predicament he was in, he had to smile. This is why he loved sniping. It was a game of chess with rifles. The next shot could be a matter of checkmate.

Von Stenger could have waited all day—he was on a dry patch of land. The American was standing in water—it was not a position a man could hold for long, no matter how tough he was. However, the increasing sound of gunfire was a reminder that the attack on Bienville was growing in intensity. It was only a matter of time before the tank shells began to rain into the flooded fields, and Von Stenger did not wish to be around when that happened.

A plan began to take shape. *My move.*

Working himself backward, one inch at a time, Von Stenger slipped back into the water. Making not so much as a ripple, he began to wade to the right of the island and then toward the causeway. His plan was to approach the American sniper from the side and surprise him.

A couple of factors worked in his favor. The first was that the American sniper's attention and the narrow field of the rifle scope would all be on the area around where the decoy body lay. He would not take his eyes off that. The second factor was the glare on the water that would mask Von Stenger's movements like the best sort of camouflage. Finally, he still had the length of plastic tubing in his pocket. He took it out now and put it in his mouth, and then slipped beneath the water while keeping his rifle held just above the surface. With the glare and some luck, it would look like a piece of wood.

* * *

COLE KEPT the scope trained on the island. The enemy had tricked him into shooting a corpse. But he had to be somewhere nearby.

He heard a sound on the bank to his right. He took his eye off the sight long enough to watch incredulously as Jolie slid down the side of the causeway and climbed into the wooden rowboat. What the hell was she doing? Looking for him? He groaned.

If he moved, if he tried to warn her, he had no doubt that the German sniper would shoot him. And then he would shoot Jolie. The German wouldn't dare give away his position by taking a shot at Jolie. Why bother? The German was after him, not Jolie.

The sounds of fighting increased as the Germans advanced toward town. A tank shell landed in the streets, exploded. Another overshot the town and landed in the marsh, blasting water and mud high into the sky. The shock wave was like a door slamming in your face.

Cole was still debating what to do when, incredibly, a figure rose up out of the water near the boat.

The German.

* * *

VON STENGER MOVED in the general direction of the causeway. The water was not all that deep, so by crouching down he was able to stay submerged while keeping his feet under him. After at least ten minutes under water, when he thought he had gone far enough, he rose very slowly.

Not twenty feet away was a boat. He remembered seeing that boat on shore. At the oars was the French Resistance fighter who had come to his room the night before. Their eyes locked. She fumbled in the bottom of the boat, started to come up with a weapon.

Von Stenger shot her.

* * *

"No!" Cole was amazed that he had actually screamed. The son of a bitch had shot Jolie. He saw the German work the bolt action and swing the rifle toward Cole's hiding place.

Cole shoved the log away and stood up, rifle raised, looked right through the scope at the German. The German was looking back at him.

Cole put the crosshairs on the German's head. He could almost feel the other sniper's crosshairs on him.

He fought the urge to fire quickly. He took a breath, held it, struggled to hold the rifle steady. The German would be doing the same. His finger took up more slack on the trigger. The crosshairs danced, came back. He was dimly aware of a tank shell screaming overhead.

When the rifle fired it came as a shock, punching into his shoulder. He saw a flash from the German's muzzle.

Then the world exploded.

HIS EARS RINGING, his nose and mouth full of mud, Cole sputtered and coughed until he could breathe. The shell from the German tank had thrown him into the water and showered him with gunk and debris from the sunken marsh.

But he was still holding the rifle. Frantically, he put it to his shoulder and scanned the marsh, looking for the German. The scope was useless, spattered with mud, but he prayed the muzzle wasn't clogged.

Nothing. Had his shot killed the German? The German had fired at him in the same instant that the Panzer shell had come screaming in. Cole's ears rang and his head throbbed, but he was fairly certain he didn't have a rifle bullet in him. His cheek did feel like it was on fire, and when he touched it his fingertips came away bloody. With a shock, he realized that's where the German's bullet had grazed him.

Goddamn close.

No time to think on that now. He had to get to

Jolie. Move, he told himself. He waded toward the boat, going as fast as the muck stirred up by the shell would allow. He could almost feel the German's crosshairs on his back and thought that each step might be his last.

Another shell ripped into the marsh, exploding not fifty feet away. Somewhere close by a heavy machine gun chattered. Being out in an open, flooded field was not a good place to be right now. It was a little too much like standing under a lone pine during a lightning storm.

He slung the rifle and struggled the last few feet, trying to run through the water. Each slogging step was like trying to lift a heavy weight with his legs. He finally reached the boat and forced himself to look inside.

He expected the worst and wasn't far wrong. Blood ran across the bottom of the skiff. He took a quick look at the wound and saw that the German's bullet had caught Jolie in the side as she was lifting her rifle—dead center, the bullet would have killed her, but it had struck a glancing blow. There was a lot of raw meat there, a lot of blood. But she was alive.

He knew he had to stop the bleeding, but first he had to get them out of there. With the Panzers advancing, the flooded marsh was about to become a killing field. Climbing into the boat would be impossible. The skiff was floating too high for him to lever himself into it, so he started pushing the boat toward dry land over at the causeway. He chanced a look back over his shoulder, still worrying about the German sniper, but the flooded field was empty.

Another Panzer shell exploded, flinging mud and water everywhere. Cole ignored that and kept moving until he got the boat to shore.

"Don't die on me, girl, you hear!"

Jolie groaned, which he took to be a good sign, but she was losing a lot of blood and she was in shock. His own mud-covered jacket and shirt were useless, so he unwound the scarf Jolie wore around her neck and stuffed it into the wound. It was the best he could do for now to staunch the bleeding.

He looked down the road toward the German position. He could see German soldiers moving forward with rifles and machine pistols, so close that he could lock eyes with them. Too close. Too goddamn close.

The entrance to the town, barricaded and defended with a .50 caliber machine gun, was only two hundred feet away. Some brave fool stood up, popped off a few shots at the Germans to drive them back, and then waved at him frantically. He realized it was Lieutenant Mulholland. There was no mistaking Mulholland's gesture. It meant *hurry up*.

Cole slung Jolie across his shoulder like a sack of oats and ran like hell.

* * *

THE EXPLOSION LIFTED Von Stenger and threw him into deeper water. He sank, his ears ringing, his eyes full of mud and grit from the blast. It happened so fast that he didn't even have a chance to get a breath before going under. He tried to swim toward the surface, but the weight of his gear held him down. The water was not deep, just a little over his head, but it was enough to drown him.

He started to flail his arms, desperate to reach the surface. What little air he had in his lungs released in a train of bubbles. *Stop.* He willed himself not to panic. Fear and panic was what got you killed. Methodically, he stripped off his tunic that had pockets weighted with shells, undid the strap of his helmet, unbuckled the utility belt that held his canteen and knife. He floated free of the muck on the bottom.

The surface was *right there,* but Von Stenger forced himself to swim a little farther away. The American was still out there. What if he was just waiting for Von Stenger to surface? He rotated and put his face out of the water, sipping air like a guppy.

When there was no slap of a bullet, he moved so that he could look toward the spot where the American had been located. He was surprised to see him moving away, toward shore, pushing the rowboat that the French girl had been in.

The American's back was too him. Such an easy shot. But Von Stenger had lost his rifle. Another shell dropped into the marsh and exploded in a geyser of mud. He could feel the shock of it through the water. Von Stenger slipped deeper into the marsh, away from the rain of shells and the stray fire coming from Bienville. *Another day,* he thought, watching the American slog toward shore.

EPILOGUE

ON JUNE 29, 1944, Lieutenant General Karl-Wilhem von Schlieben surrendered the city of Cherbourg to the Americans. The last German stronghold on the Cotentin Peninsula had fallen. The battle for Normandy that had begun before dawn nearly a month before with the assault on Omaha Beach was over.

The struggle for Cherbourg had not been easy, with nearly 3,000 Americans killed and thousands more wounded in the final days of fighting. Losses for the Germans, who had their backs to the Atlantic, were even more severe with nearly 8,000 killed or missing. In the end, almost 30,000 German troops surrendered in those last days of June. As the city fell, General Friedrich Dollman, commander of the German Seventh Army, was informed that he faced a court martial. It would never be carried out—the loss of the city brought on a heart attack and he died within hours.

Among the troops who streamed into the captured city was a trio of American snipers. Their uniforms were dirty and shredded from weeks of crawling through brambles and sleeping rough in the bocage country. Even their rifles looked battered, the sheen gone from the barrels, the paint on the scopes scratched. But the weapons retained a well-oiled, deadly appearance. Until a few days ago they had been accompanied by a certain British paratrooper, but Corporal Neville had finally rejoined his own unit.

"It's not much more than a pile of bricks," said one of the snipers, a dark-skinned Italian who was even darker after the long days of fighting in the French sun. Something else had happened to him in the field—he had become a much better shot thanks to lots and lots of practice.

"Those big Navy guns turned it to rubble," said the lieutenant. He was referring to the Allied fleet that had anchored offshore and bombarded the Germans. Anyone who had not seen the lieutenant in the last month would scarcely recognize him. He looked leaner and careworn, with permanent lines etched into his face. A bandage soaked through with dried blood was wrapped tightly around his upper left arm. He now gave direct orders without thinking twice about them. "They anchored off shore and gave them a good pounding."

"Speaking of pounding, I wonder if there are any French girls here who need a good one," the sniper said.

"Shut up, Vaccaro," the lieutenant said. By now, the words were a reflex, like shooing flies.

The third sniper walked alone, moving with an easy lope through the streets of the ruined city. He wore a Confederate flag painted on his helmet, though the image of the flag was nearly hidden by a layer of dust and grime. The helmet had a bullet hole in it.

Though Cole was more at home in the woods and fields, he had seen enough ruined towns that he was familiar with what to expect. St. Lo, Caen, Carentan, Bienville—he had been through more than a few of those towns that most Americans had never heard of until a few weeks ago, and now they would never forget.

The sniper's eyes never stopped moving across the roof tops and the upper windows of the half-ruined houses. Unlike the others, his rifle was held at the ready so that he could put it to his shoulder in an instant. It just so happened that he still carried a Mauser.

They had been operating as a counter sniper unit,

fighting mostly on their own, for weeks now. Sniper warfare across the bocage had been vicious, mainly because what they increasingly encountered was a variety of SS sniper that did not move strategically, but who buried himself like a tick. He occupied a sniper nest with a supply of ammunition and rations, and stayed until he was killed—or sometimes captured. Sadly, most of these stubborn German snipers were teenage boys who were so brainwashed about heroism and the glory of defending the Fatherland that they fought to the death. Unfortunately, they took the lives of too many Allied troops first.

Cole often wondered about the Ghost Sniper. *Das Gespenst*. Had he died in that flooded marsh? That was only weeks ago, but it seemed like years. Cole would have liked to have searched for the body, but the fighting had been too fierce for that. He could only trust that his bullet had struck home.

There had been reports of a sniper who operated in a way much different from the young SS fanatics. Outside Caen, this sniper had pinned down a large American unit, causing many casualties before slipping away. Similar sniper attacks had decimated an entire company on the approach to Cherbourg just a couple of days before.

Das Gespenst? The thought nagged at Cole. If the Ghost Sniper wasn't dead, it was unfinished business.

Jolie Molyneaux had survived being shot, but she

was still recovering in an Allied hospital. If this Von Stenger was still alive, Cole reckoned he owed it to Jolie to kill him. Revenge wasn't a casual idea to someone like Micajah Cole—the notion of it coursed through his veins like blood.

"How come you never tell Cole to shut up, Lieutenant?" Vaccaro asked. "He never stops talking. You'd think he was trying to talk the goddamn Germans to death."

"Shut up, Vaccaro," Cole said.

The snipers moved on through the ruined city. Huge numbers of captured Germans moved in the opposite direction, their hands locked behind their heads, weary GIs marching beside them with weapons at the ready. Though the victors marched alongside the defeated, it was hard to say which side looked more exhausted.

"Where to next, Lieutenant?" Vaccaro asked. It just wasn't in his nature to shut up.

The lieutenant stopped and looked around at the streets, now filled with American troops and German prisoners. A few French civilians had ventured out, looking with dismay and wonder at the piles of bricks and the broken streets. Beyond the town they could see the harbor, filled with American Navy ships. Someone had raised an American and a French flag in the city square. They snapped side by side in the breeze off the sea.

"I'd say we're done here," the lieutenant announced. He smiled. "So what's next? Germany. I'd say we're on our way to Germany."

*　*　*

DESPITE THE DEFEAT and surrender of Cherbourg, not all the German troops on the Cotentin Peninsula had been captured. It was too big a place and there were too many woods and fields in which to elude the enemy.

Those who were left were now joining the retreat across the Seine into Belgium, dodging Allied aircraft and patrols.

A truck carrying battle-hardened Wehrmacht troops rolled down a dirt road through the countryside. Up ahead, a lone figure in a German uniform emerged from the woods and stood in the road, forcing the truck to stop.

Puzzled, the driver leaned out the window. He was surprised to see that the soldier carried a sniper's rifle with a telescopic sight and that he wore a captain's uniform. In the Wehrmacht, there were a few legendary soldiers, known for their bravery or prowess. With a start, the driver realized this must be the Ghost Sniper he had heard about.

"Are you on your way to fight or surrender?" the lone sniper asked.

"We are going to fight," the driver said. His face was grim and determined. "The *Amis* have not won yet."

"Do you have room for one more?"

"Of course, *Herr Hauptmann*. Do you wish to ride up front, sir? We can make room."

"Thank you, but the back is fine."

The sniper walked around and climbed in, taking care with the rifle and its telescopic sight, which he had been lucky to find on the battlefield after losing his prized Mosin-Nagant in the marshes around Bienville. He nodded at the grizzled German troops sitting there on benches. Then the truck lurched into gear and drove off toward Belgium.

-Das Ende-

HISTORICAL NOTE

Back in the 1990s I had the opportunity to spend some time interviewing D-Day veterans for a series of newspaper articles. Many of these men went ashore at Omaha Beach with the 29th Division, but a few of the men I interviewed were paratroopers, Coast Guardsmen who crewed landing craft, and even a clerk or two armed with typewriters. While I've read several books to gain a better understanding of D-Day operations, it's really these first-hand accounts of men who were there in 1944 that have helped in creating the details of the Normandy campaign. Several of the incidents and descriptions of events come from their narratives. Experts on the Normandy campaign will see that I have taken some liberties in combining the events and geography of

Carentan and Angoville au Plain in the final encounter between the Germans, Americans and British, at the fictional town of Bienville.

—D.H.